Fiona stood in the center of the room, bound to one of several thick wooden pillars with her hands above her head. Her dress was torn nearly to her waist and her shapely legs were scratched and bruised, but she held her chin high, eyes blazing. The pillar to which she had been tied was bristling with throwing knives, their wicked points buried in the ancient wood all around her. The rider in the fur hat stood before her, now revealed as a tall, brutish man with long gray hair, a sharp forked beard and an expression of avid hunger. The man held several knives in one large hand like a deadly bouquet. He transferred one to his empty hand, then smiled and licked his lips.

"I told you . . ." Fiona began to say.

The man raised his elbow to the ceiling and then brought his arm swiftly downward, letting the knife fly. It sank deep into the wood a bare millimeter from Fiona's temple. She yelped as she tried to twist away and found her head trapped, a thick lock of her hair pinned to the wood by the blade.

Gabriel's hand reflexively drew his Colt. The man in the fur hat switched another knife to his empty hand.

Gabriel raised the Colt so its barrel was aimed directly at the knife thrower's forehead. He called out: "Put the knives down and let her go."

With stunning speed, the man spun and let the blade fly in Gabriel's direction . . .

Enjoy these other Gabriel Hunt adventures:

**HUNT AT THE WELL OF ETERNITY
HUNT THROUGH THE CRADLE OF FEAR
HUNT AT WORLD'S END
HUNT AMONG THE KILLERS OF MEN ***
HUNT THROUGH NAPOLEON'S WEB *

* coming soon

GABRIEL HUNT

HUNT

Beyond the Frozen Fire

AS TOLD TO CHRISTA FAUST

LEISURE BOOKS NEW YORK CITY

A LEISURE BOOK®

April 2010

Published by

Dorchester Publishing Co., Inc.
200 Madison Avenue
New York, NY 10016

in collaboration with Winterfall LLC

ISBN 10: 0-8439-6247-X
ISBN 13: 978-0-8439-6247-5
E-ISBN: 978-1-4285-0829-3

GABRIEL HUNT was created by Charles Ardai and is a trademark of Winterfall LLC.

The name "Leisure Books" and the stylized "L" with design are trademarks of Dorchester Publishing Co., Inc.

Printed in the United States of America.

10 9 8 7 6 5 4 3 2 1

Visit us online at www.dorchesterpub.com or
www.HuntForAdventure.com

HUNT

Beyond the Frozen Fire

Chapter 1

"I'd ask what a nice girl like you is doing in a place like this," Gabriel told the brunette sitting at the bar with her back to him. "But I already know exactly what you're doing."

The brunette spun, reaching for the revolver beside her glass, but Gabriel grabbed her wrist before she could raise it to draw a bead between his eyes.

"I also know you're not a very nice girl," Gabriel said, tightening his grip and meeting her furious gaze without flinching.

The bar was a murky, nameless Moldovan hole-in-the-wall, spitting distance from the Transdniestrian border. The angry brunette was Dr. Fiona Rush, professor in Cambridge University's prestigious archeology department and partner in Gabriel Hunt's latest Eastern European expedition. She had also been Gabriel's lover, which made it all the worse when she'd double-crossed him and run off with the legendary jewel-encrusted Cossack dagger they'd come here to find. There were some who claimed that the *kindjal* was cursed, that it would bring sorrow and strife to anyone who possessed it. After everything he'd been through in the past few days, Gabriel was inclined to agree.

When Gabriel grabbed Fiona's wrist, all conversation around them abruptly ceased. Several men nearby, taller even than Gabriel and twice as wide, raised weapons and cold, hostile glares and aimed both in Gabriel's direction. For a tense stretch of seconds, nothing happened. A Romanian melody fought its way through the static on a cheap transistor radio behind the bar. The ancient, toothless bartender suddenly remembered something critical that needed to be done right away in the storeroom in the back. Gabriel silently tried to decide which of the armed men posed the most serious threat and to measure where they were located in relation to both the front and back doors. He did not let go of Fiona's wrist.

Fiona shook her head, offering a few curt words in Romanian. The thugs pocketed their various weapons, some more reluctantly than others. They all continued to stare at Gabriel with undisguised hostility. It was clear it wouldn't take much for the weapons to reappear. Gabriel let Fiona go, but stayed alert and wary.

"Have a drink," Fiona said, casually, as if she'd just happened to run into an old friend. She took an extra glass from the rack above the bar and poured a generous knock of the rich Moldovan brandy known as *divin*. "You must be thirsty."

"I don't want a drink," Gabriel said, pushing the glass away. "I want the *kindjal*."

"You're not still cross about that, are you?" Fiona smiled and topped off her own glass from the dusty bottle. "Honestly, it was nothing personal."

"Did you think you could just cut me out and sell to the highest bidder?" Gabriel asked. "That dagger is a significant historical artifact. It should be on display in a museum, not locked up by some rich collector. You of all people ought to know that."

"You know what your problem is, Gabriel?" Fiona arched a dark eyebrow. "You're still laboring under this charmingly anachronistic sense of right and wrong. This is the twenty-first century. You need to be more . . ." She took a sip of her *divin* and looked up at Gabriel with the sultry gaze that had gotten him into this trouble in the first place. "More flexible."

"No more games, Fiona," Gabriel said. "I know you're planning on meeting your buyer in this bar, but I also know you're too smart to have the *kindjal* on hand for the negotiation. So where is it?"

"We could split the money," Fiona said, dropping a hand to Gabriel's thigh. "We can just claim the *kindjal* was stolen. That sort of thing happens all the time in this part of the world. No one will ever be the wiser."

"Where is it?" Gabriel asked again, pushing her hand away. "I'm asking nicely. Next time I ask, it won't be so nice."

"You really are going to be tedious about this, aren't you?" Fiona sighed and emptied her glass, but when she tried for another refill, she found the bottle empty. "Fine, I'll take you to it. But first let's have one more drink, shall we? For old time's sake."

She gestured to the bartender, who had tentatively crept back to his post when it appeared there would be no violence after all. Holding her glass up high, she called out something in Romanian that caused the entire bar to turn her way. Amazingly, the chilly scowls all melted into broad, gap-toothed smiles. Glasses were raised all around and suddenly Gabriel was surrounded by thick, strapping men slapping him on the back and shaking his hand.

"What the hell did you say to them?" Gabriel asked, searching for Fiona between the moving mountain range of giant shoulders and flushed, grinning faces. Romanian was one of the few Eastern European languages he didn't speak even a cursory amount of.

"I told them drinks were on you," Fiona said with a smirk as the bartender obligingly opened a bottle of vodka and began filling upraised glasses. "I also said that you were a big American movie director from Hollywood looking for Moldovans to cast in your new picture."

An enormous ox with a blond beard suddenly pulled Gabriel into an aromatic bear hug as if he were a long lost brother. Someone began singing a patriotic song loud and off key and the ox enthusiastically joined in, slapping Gabriel's back so hard it nearly knocked him off his feet. Another equally large but beardless man tapped Gabriel on the shoulder and began demonstrating a terrifyingly drunken knife trick on the bar, weaving the blade back and forth between fat sausage fingers.

Gabriel tried to keep Fiona in view, but she vanished between two of the bar's larger patrons.

Gabriel pressed far too many Moldovan *lei* into the astonished bartender's hand and bullied his way through the crowd toward the open back door. He was almost waylaid by a pair of eager Moldovans clamoring for their free drink, but he managed to break free and make it to the door. When he burst through, he found himself in a narrow alley barely wide enough to accommodate his shoulders. He heard the clatter of horses' hooves approaching. There was only one streetlight in this remote village and, in typical Moldovan fashion, it had been turned off to save money. The only illumination came from the large, nearly full moon behind swift-moving clouds.

As his eyes adjusted to the dark, he spotted Fiona's distinctive silhouette at the mouth of the alley and called out her name. She turned toward him just as the moon slipped out from behind the clouds, pale silvery light glinting off the steel barrel of her pistol.

Gabriel dove for cover, tasting brick dust as a bullet smashed into the wall inches from where his head had been. He unholstered his Colt Peacemaker and risked a glance at the mouth of the alley just in time to see a massive white horse thunder into view. The rider reached effortlessly down and grabbed Fiona's narrow waist, hauling her up and across the saddle. She let out a breathless shriek and before Gabriel could blink, the horse, its rider and Fiona were gone.

Chapter 2

Gabriel swore under his breath and ran out to the mouth of the alley. He could barely make out the ghostly white shape of the horse swiftly galloping down the muddy road. But he could hear Fiona continuing to scream, her voice dwindling with distance.

Not quite the escape she'd intended, Gabriel thought, and for a moment he was tempted to simply let Fiona go to whatever awful fate awaited. She had, after all, betrayed him. More than that—she'd just tried to kill him. But damn it, she was the only one who knew where the *kindjal* was hidden . . . and even after everything she'd put him through, his conscience wouldn't let him just stand by and let her be abducted, maybe tortured to reveal the *kindjal*'s location. Maybe worse.

His Gypsy driver, Djordji, already had the cranky, Cold War–era Russian jeep running when Gabriel vaulted into the passenger seat without opening the door. "Follow that horse," Gabriel muttered. Djordji reacted without comment, as poker-faced and nonchalant as if he had been asked to drive to another pub.

As the jeep accelerated along the deeply rutted, unpaved road, the fleeing horse vanished around a corner.

When the jeep reached and rounded the same corner, Gabriel was surprised to see not one but several horses on the road ahead. The white stallion had the lead, its rider wearing a tall, distinctive fur hat. Gabriel could see Fiona's long pale legs kicking frantically off to one side of the saddle. The other horses looked brown or black— hard to tell in the darkness—and were being ridden by smaller men, hunched close to their horses' necks. They raced past a large, decrepit building that may once have been a stable but was now surrounded by rusted wrecks of farm equipment and the carcass of a Volkswagen bus. Another turn in the road loomed and the horses swung around it in a pack. Djordji floored the gas and moments later roared into the turn, engine screaming. But when they came out on the other side, the only things visible down the road were the distant yellow lights of the Transdniestrian border crossing. The horses were gone.

"Stop," Gabriel said. Djordji laid on the brakes and they squealed to a halt in the middle of the road. Gabriel held up a finger for silence. The clattering of hooves came to them quietly from the left. Gabriel squinted and scanned the dark terrain off to the side of the road. It was an empty field—but near the horizon he could just make out several figures pounding desperately away.

"There," he said, pointing.

Djordji stepped on the gas and wrenched the wheel hard to the left, taking the jeep off the road and into the field. It was rocky and lined with the dry stalks of some crop that clearly hadn't fared well during the past season. The bone-jarring jolts of the jeep's balding tires traveling over the furrowed field threatened to throw both of them out of the car.

As they drew closer to the fleeing riders, a volley of bullets ricocheted off the jeep's dented olive flank. Gabriel unholstered his Colt and returned fire without hesitation, but the uneven ground, the dark and the distance made accurate shooting next to impossible. Luckily this handicap went both ways.

"Try and hold her steady," he told Djordji, and he stood up in the open-topped jeep, bracing himself against the windshield and aiming at the rearmost rider, who was still twenty yards ahead of them and off to one side. Gabriel fired off a single shot but the jeep hit a rock and the shot went hopelessly wide. He swore and urged Djordji to close the distance. The taciturn Gypsy made a sour face under his thick white mustache.

"Is jeep," he said. "Not race car."

Gabriel ignored the comment and tried to steady his aim, fighting the uneven rhythm of bumps and dips. He slowly blew all the air out of his lungs and when the jeep hit a miraculously smooth patch of ground, he squeezed the trigger. This time the last rider in the pack went down. His now riderless horse slowed from a gallop to a trot as Djordji pulled the jeep up alongside.

Most of the horses Gabriel had seen around the local villages were pretty sorry specimens. Bony, spavined and morose, seemingly as resigned to their disappointing lot in life as their gloomy Moldovan masters. But this muscular chestnut mare was absolutely stunning. Proud, sleek and obviously quite expensive. A Ferrari of a horse. It made Gabriel wonder about her owner, but he didn't have time to wonder for long. Because it turned out that the beautiful horse was not riderless after all.

Apparently the rider hadn't been shot—he'd simply dropped down on the far side of the horse to avoid

Gabriel's bullet, clinging to the tack and keeping the horse's body between him and the jeep. Now he swung back up, leaping effortlessly to his feet in the saddle. In the moonlight Gabriel could see the rider's pale, angry face and shaved head with its long traditional Cossack forelock. He stood on the horse's back with a comfortable, loose-limbed stance like a surfer riding a wave.

The next thing Gabriel knew, the rider had leapt from the horse and knocked him into the backseat, a gleaming blade slashing the air inches from his face. Gabriel's Colt tumbled from his grip and onto the floor of the jeep.

Gabriel swiftly grabbed the Cossack's knife hand and smashed it as hard as he could against the frame of the front seat. The Cossack bared his teeth and refused to drop the knife, so Gabriel dug the tip of his thumb into the soft underside of the Cossack's wrist and gave his hand a few more knocks against the metal frame.

The jeep hit a rocky bump that sent it airborne for several seconds. The Cossack grunted and let go of the knife, clinging to Gabriel as they were bounced together into the air like ingredients in a chef's sauté pan. When the jeep hit the ground, the grappling men slammed back down to the floor. The Cossack's forehead smashed against Gabriel's and the passenger-side back door flipped open. It snapped off as Djordji sideswiped a sturdy tree. The Cossack's knife skittered across the floor and out of the jeep. He lunged for it, too late. Then he saw Gabriel's fallen pistol sliding along the floor and went for it instead. Gabriel swung a stiff elbow, cracking the Cossack in the jaw. The man's head snapped back and Gabriel reached for the Colt himself, but the jeep made a sharp right and the gun slid away, under the driver's seat.

Wiping a trail of blood from his split lip, the rider got up into a crouch and threw a short kick at Gabriel, his dusty boot narrowly missing Gabriel's face. Gabriel scrambled to his feet and threw a hard right, but the jeep hit another nasty bump and he found himself over-balanced, falling halfway out the broken back door, facedown, hands scrambling for purchase. The rider was on top of him in an instant, belly to back, gripping a fistful of Gabriel's hair. A flood of hot, suffocating exhaust from the tailpipe blew into Gabriel's face as the rider pushed Gabriel's head toward the spinning rear wheel.

Spangles danced in the borders of Gabriel's vision and he felt his head go fuzzy from the fumes. He knew he had to act fast. His right cheek was less than an inch from the muddy wheel. Gripping one of the bars of the jeep's frame in one hand, he reached back and seized the rider's dangling forelock with the other. As the jeep swerved, Gabriel yanked down-ward on the braided hair while pushing up against the man's chest with his shoulders and hips. The rider went over, flipping out of the jeep—but as he went, he managed to wrap his arms tightly around Gabriel's chest. Gabriel felt himself dragged out of the speeding car. He clung desperately onto the bar he'd grabbed hold of, his arm nearly wrenching from its socket. The rider, meanwhile, clung desperately to Gabriel, sliding down along his body until he was holding tightly to Gabriel's waist. Gabriel looked back at the furious Cossack. He was being dragged along the ground but holding on.

Djordji, meanwhile, kept speeding along, either oblivious to what was going on behind him or convinced that following Gabriel's last instruction, to catch up with the other horses, was the best way he could be helpful.

Gabriel slammed his heel into the Cossack's knee-cap. The Cossack grunted but would not let go. Glancing to the side, Gabriel saw they were approaching a wide, rocky stream. He called out to Djordji.

"Drive into the water!"

Djordji swung the steering wheel and seconds later they plunged headlong into the icy stream. Gabriel's face stayed barely above the surface, but the rider beneath him was completely submerged. Tough bastard that he was, he still managed to hang on, but Gabriel felt the grip around his waist loosen. Gabriel pulled his legs up and gave the man a savage kick. This finally dislodged him, and, freed of the excess weight, Gabriel was able to haul himself back up into the jeep. Behind him, he saw the rider rise to his knees, cursing, in the middle of the stream. The jeep squelched through the mud and climbed the opposite bank, leaving the Cossack in the distance.

"Is not good," Djordji said when Gabriel climbed, dripping, into the front seat.

Gabriel figured his driver could have been talking about any number of things. "What's not good?"

"They cross to Transdniestria," Djordji said, pointing to the remaining riders galloping ahead of them. As Gabriel watched, the white stallion and one of the other horses jumped across what appeared to be a deep, rocky ravine. "Jeep cannot go that way. We have to go around."

But Gabriel knew they couldn't go around—by the time they made it, all signs of the horses and riders would be gone.

"We're not going around," Gabriel said. "Speed up."

Djordji looked at him as if he had lost his mind, but kept his foot on the gas. They were just yards from the edge of the ravine.

Gabriel reached down into the footwell, groped around till he found his Colt, and reholstered it. "Get me next to one of those horses," he said, standing up again. He climbed onto the seat.

A third rider reached the ravine and leapt across. There were only two left. As Djordji poured on what additional speed remained in the jeep's overtaxed engine, they overtook the last horse. The rider looked to his side. He seemed surprised to see Gabriel there, standing beside him. Gabriel cocked a smile at him, and the man smiled back. *"Dobry vecher, gospodin,"* Gabriel said, and swung a wide right into the rider's face, knocking him backward off his horse. Gabriel looked ahead. There were only seconds left before they hit the ravine. Gabriel leapt astride the now empty saddle and swept the reins up in his hands.

Djordji slammed on the brakes, bringing the jeep to a halt in a massive cloud of dust, just inches from the lip of the ravine. Gabriel gripped the black mare's steaming flanks with his legs and pulled back on the reins, urging the animal to make the jump.

The horse let out a snort of protest against her new, unfamiliar rider but launched herself across the ravine after her fellows. There was a tense moment of shifting pebbles and slipping hooves as they landed on the far side and the horse fought to maintain her balance. Gabriel leaned forward and spurred his anxious mount ahead. She regained her footing and took off after the other riders.

As the horse galloped across the moonlit steppe, their destination came into view. An ancient ruin of a large circular fortress, grim, brooding half-hidden by the low broken hills around it. This was no tourist attraction, no spectacular gothic castle out of a travel brochure. It was an ugly, forgotten place, nothing left but cold, unfriendly walls designed not for aesthetics but function, the function being to keep enemies out. But the defenses had been breached centuries ago, and enemies or not, the Cossacks were riding in.

As they approached the fortress, a heavy, rusted portcullis slowly cranked open, allowing the riders to pass beneath and into the dull yellow glow emanating from the interior. As the portcullis began to close, Gabriel urged his mount to top speed.

He wasn't going to be able to make it on horseback, he saw—the metal gate was dropping too quickly, and already there was no room. Yanking the reins sharply to the right, Gabriel dropped off the horse to his left, diving to the ground and rolling beneath the portcullis' descending spikes. As the ancient gate slammed closed, Gabriel could feel one leg of his pants catch and tear. He struggled to stand and pull his pant leg free from the spike that had pinned it to the ground. There was a loud rip as he freed himself, but the sound was drowned out by a louder ratcheting sound, a sound of metal sliding against metal that made his heart sink when he heard it. He spun to face the interior of the fortress and found himself staring into the business ends of over a dozen AK-47s.

Chapter 3

Gabriel could see the white horse standing by the open doorway of a low stone building on the opposite side of the courtyard. Steep stone steps were visible through the doorway, leading sharply down into the darkness beyond, but Fiona and the rider who had grabbed her—the man with the tall fur hat—were nowhere in sight.

However there was no time to contemplate where Fiona might have been taken, because Gabriel was distracted by the infinitely more pressing issue of the hostile, rifle-wielding soldiers currently drawing down on him.

One of their number, a handsome, dark-haired older man with the insignia of a commanding officer, stepped forward and ordered Gabriel, in Russian, to surrender his gun. One of the younger soldiers helpfully clarified the command by tapping Gabriel's shoulder holster with the barrel of his Kalashnikov and then jamming the muzzle into the soft spot under Gabriel's ear.

Gabriel raised his hands and slowly removed the Colt from its holster. His eyes desperately scanned his surroundings for any hope of escape. There were stacks of stenciled wooden crates, several parked military vehicles and a pair of noisy, foul-smelling generators powering the strings of weak yellow lightbulbs that illuminated the scene. The remaining riders had dismounted at the far end of the courtyard and were seeing to their horses with only the vaguest interest in Gabriel's predicament. A group of grim-faced African men in suits were standing to his left, conversing quietly in French and giving him occasional stony glares while one of their number counted the crates, jotting figures on a clipboard. The surrounding walls were over twenty feet high. There was no visible way out.

Gabriel held his pistol out at arm's length and tossed it to the ground. It slid across the mossy paving stones and came to rest against the commanding officer's spit-shined shoe. The soldier pressing his rifle against Gabriel's neck backed off with a smug look. The smugness rapidly transformed to curiosity, then astonishment as the sound of an approaching vehicle became a deafening crash. Djordji's jeep rammed the rusty portcullis, knocking it loose from its ancient moorings and driving into the courtyard with the gate drunkenly balanced across the hood, steam billowing from the damaged engine.

Gabriel leapt aside, narrowly avoiding being flattened as the jeep scattered men before it like bowling pins. He dove for his Colt, rolling away with the gun in hand and ending up behind a stack of wooden crates. Gabriel ducked down and listened to the multilingual chaos, trying to discern Djordji's fate while his fingers moved on autopilot, emptying the Colt's spent brass and reloading. He'd only had time to slide two fresh slugs into the cylinder when a wiry young soldier dropped down on him from the stack of crates above, slamming a fist into the back of his neck and causing the remaining bullets in Gabriel's palm to drop and scatter.

Gabriel swore, twisting and bringing the hand holding the pistol up toward his attacker, but the Russian grabbed Gabriel's hand and pressed his thumb against the still open cylinder to keep it from snapping shut. Gabriel managed to wrench his hand free from the Russian's grip, but not before the struggle caused the two bullets to slip from the chamber and roll away under one of the crates. He let the young Russian have it in the temple with the butt of the empty gun. The Russian dropped as if suddenly boneless. Stepping over his crumpled form, Gabriel angrily holstered the empty Colt and peered around the stack of crates.

The courtyard was full of soldiers, running and shouting. The jeep was upside down and on fire, but Djordji wasn't in it. In fact, he was nowhere in sight. Several men were battling the smoky blaze with foam extinguishers while others, under the supervision of the grim Africans, formed lines to swiftly move crates of ammo and other dangerous explosives away from the fire. It was then that Gabriel realized what was going on here. Clearly he had stumbled into the middle of some kind of arms deal. But what did this have to do with Fiona and the *kindjal*?

Gabriel eyed the open door and the stone steps down which Fiona and her captor had disappeared. He thought he had a clear shot and was about to make a run for it when one of the Africans came around the far corner of the stack of crates. His eyes widened in surprise and then narrowed to a slit as he pulled out an HK .45, drawing a bead on Gabriel's chest.

Gabriel raised his palms till they framed his face. In heavily accented French, the African told Gabriel to prepare for death. Gabriel responded in the same tongue. "You might want to do a little preparation yourself," he said.

"I? For what?" The man sneered. "I have the gun in my hand, and you have nothing."

"Yes," Gabriel said, "but my friend there, behind you, has a shovel."

The man got the beginning of a contemptuous laugh out before the shovel in Djordji's hands slammed into the back of his head with a loud crack. The man staggered and crumpled, clutching at the crates as he fell. One toppled onto him, breaking open when it struck the ground. A pair of smooth, spherical hand grenades spilled out.

Gabriel snatched one up. "Nobody move!" he shouted. He stepped out into view with his finger through the pin loop. "Drop your weapons."

There was a moment of shocked silence and then a ripple of outraged Russian murmurs.

"You wouldn't dare," replied the dark-haired officer who'd first confronted Gabriel.

"Of course I would," Gabriel replied in Russian. "Grenade or gun, I'm just as dead, but this way I get to take some of you with me." The logic seemed to sink in, and the officer took a step back. Gabriel motioned for Djordji to join him as he moved sideways toward the open door.

Every pair of eyes in the courtyard was focused on Gabriel as weapons were lowered but not dropped. The look on the officer's face was one of barely suppressed rage. Gabriel closed the last few feet between him and the door.

"Go," he said to Djordji, gesturing for the Gypsy to start down the stone steps.

While the older man descended, Gabriel stood in the open doorway, his finger on the pin of the hand grenade. Once he could no longer hear Djordji's steps, Gabriel called to the officer. "Here. Catch." He made as if to throw the grenade at the man, who ducked away in fear—but at the last instant, Gabriel spun and slung the grenade sidelong toward the nearest stack of munitions.

The hot fist of the ensuing explosion shoved Gabriel backward into the stairway. Gabriel pulled the heavy wooden door closed, sliding a massive iron bar into place to seal it. He could hear the firecracker sound of explosions and gunshots, then a barrage of angry Russian as the soldiers beat their fists and gun butts against the door. Gabriel raced downward, following the path Djordji had taken—and Fiona before him—into the bowels of the ancient fortress.

He met up with Djordji halfway down. The Gypsy was leaning against the stone wall, the shovel still gripped in one fist. Djordji put the index finger of his other hand to his lips and gestured with his head below them, where the stone steps vanished into darkness. There were voices below, one male and one female, both furious.

"*Where?*" the man's voice thundered in heavily accented English. "*You tell, now!*"

"*I don't know where it is,*" Fiona shouted back, unconvincingly. "*I swear I don't.*"

Gabriel took the lead and walked silently, cautiously, down the steps. As they crept around a turn, the darkness was replaced by a dim flickering light, the startlingly red glow a shade Gabriel remembered seeing only once before, in a Croatian monastery; when he'd asked what accounted for the unusual color of the flame, they'd explained it was the admixture of the tallow with a portion of ground-up human bone. The calcium, they explained. Calcium burns brick red.

Gabriel still couldn't see anything before him—there was another curve in the steps ahead—but he could make out a distinct and repetitive sound, a kind of sharp, resonant *thwack*, followed swiftly each time by a high-pitched feminine gasp.

He hastened ahead to the curve, Djordji just steps behind. When they came around it, the candlelit scene was revealed. Fiona stood in the center of a large, low-ceilinged room, bound to one of several thick wooden pillars with her hands above her head. Her dress was torn nearly to her waist and her shapely legs were scratched and bruised, but she held her small, defiant chin high, eyes blazing. The pillar to which she had been tied was bristling with throwing knives, their wicked points buried in the ancient wood all around her bound and squirming form. The rider in the fur hat stood before her, now revealed as a tall, brutish man with long gray hair, a sharp forked beard and an expression of avid hunger that might have been lust or greed or religious zeal, or perhaps a combination of all three. The man held several knives in one large hand like a deadly bouquet, the same sort of knives that currently surrounded Fiona's tense, quivering body. He transferred one to his empty hand, then smiled and licked his lips.

"I told you . . ." Fiona began to say.

The man in the fur hat raised his elbow to the ceiling and then brought his arm swiftly downward, letting the knife fly. It sank deep into the wood a bare millimeter from Fiona's temple. She yelped as she tried to twist away and found her head trapped, a thick lock of her hair pinned to the wood by the blade.

Gabriel's hand reflexively drew the now empty Colt. He looked to Djordji and motioned for the Gypsy to hand him the shovel. Should he charge the man with the shovel? Try to bluff with the gun? He needed to act fast, because the next strike of a blade could be fatal. Behind him, Djordji silently crossed himself. The man in the fur hat switched another knife to his empty hand. Gabriel looked from the shovel to the gun and back again.

"Ah, hell," he muttered, then raised the Colt so its barrel was aimed directly at the knife thrower's forehead. He called out: "Put the knives down and let her go."

With stunning speed, the man spun and let the blade fly in Gabriel's direction. Gabriel's reflexes were barely quick enough for him to bring the head of the shovel up into the knife's path. The blade rang loudly against the metal of the shovel, then ricocheted off, burying itself to the hilt in the dirt between two slabs of stone at the foot of the stairs.

Gabriel charged down the remaining steps as the man readied for another throw. Gabriel felt level ground beneath his feet and saw a second knife spinning toward him, end over end. He swung the shovel, deflecting it. He saw Djordji duck as the knife passed by him. The Gypsy flattened himself against the nearest wall, then darted away into the safety of the shadows.

The knife thrower stepped back to Fiona's side, one of the remaining knives clutched in each hand. He held one up in throwing position and swung the other to a point directly below her chin. "You come," he said, "I carve."

Gabriel drew to a halt, gun raised. "You move, I shoot."

"This close," the man said softly, "blade is faster." And to demonstrate he took a nick out of Fiona's throat with a minute twitch of his wrist. A drop of blood formed, then a trail, a line of red reaching down toward her collarbone. Fiona didn't make a sound, but Gabriel could see the pain and fear in her eyes.

Was a blade faster than a bullet? It depended on circumstances and was a question tacticians could debate. But a real blade was definitely faster than a non-existent bullet.

Gabriel lowered his gun. "All right," he said. "You win. I'll tell you where the *kindjal* is."

"You?" the man said, his eyes narrowing with disbelief.

"Me," Gabriel said. "She passed it to me in the bar. I hid it in the alleyway."

The man considered this for a moment, then shook his head. "You lie. You lie to save woman." He leered. "Because you like, no?"

"No," Gabriel said. "I don't like. I did once, very much. But that was a long time ago." He saw the change in Fiona's expression. The look of pain in her eyes was due to more now than just the blade at her throat.

"Then why," the man said, "do you try to save her?"

"Because," Gabriel said, "that's what I do."

The knife thrower turned then, at a sound beside him, but not before Djordji, who had crept along the shadows of the wall and circled around behind him, was able to lunge forward and seize the man in a crushing bear hug. They grappled, the knife thrower straining mightily to free his arms, which Djordji held pinned to his sides. Gabriel ran forward, the shovel swinging in a wide arc. The rust-stained metal caught the knife thrower full in the face, sending the fur hat flying. The man went limp in Djordji's grip. The Gypsy let him go, and he slid to the floor.

"Thank you," Gabriel said. "That was—"

"Gabriel!" Fiona cried. "Look out!"

The bone-jarring roar of a high caliber gunshot made Gabriel leap backward. Djordji uttered a whispered Romany oath and, to Gabriel's horror, collapsed first to his knees and then onto his side, a dark stain spreading across the shoulder of his bright red shirt.

Gabriel dropped to the ground beside him. Djordji was still conscious, but his breaths were suddenly rapid and shallow and his face was pale and wet with cold sweat. Blood pooled on the stone beneath him.

A reedy voice issued from the shadows at the far side of the room. "You . . . must be the famous Gabriel Hunt."

Chapter 4

Gabriel looked up. He saw a small, dapper man in an immaculate suit come forward. The man had an expressionless, oddly doll-like face and he was holding an enormous, showy chrome Desert Eagle, his finger tight on the trigger.

"Permit me to introduce myself," the dapper man said. His accent sounded Ukrainian. "I am Vladislav Shevchenko. I, too, have an interest in . . ." He paused, as if searching for the right English word. "Antiquities. Do not get me wrong, it is not my primary trade. My primary trade is the one you saw upstairs, the trade in modern weapons. But there is no . . . elegance to a modern weapon. You press a button, a man dies, a car explodes—there is no grace there, no beauty. The money, however, it is good. This . . . lucrative trade in inelegant modern armaments allows me to collect rarer, dare I say unique, items such as the one we have both been searching for."

He stepped forward, the gun not wavering by so much as an inch.

"Imagine my sense of betrayal and disappointment when I heard that Dr. Rush here was planning to sell the object of our common interest to one of my most bitter rivals. I suspect it was not very different from your emotions when you discovered she had betrayed you."

He took another step closer, flat black shark eyes absorbing the crimson firelight and reflecting nothing. "I hope we can understand each other, Mr. Hunt. Maybe you will be more reasonable than our mutual lady-friend. I daresay you owe me something in any event, given the . . . damage you've done to my other transaction." He gestured toward the ceiling with his head. "I feel that it is the least you can do to make amends."

"He doesn't know where the *kindjal* is, you bastard," Fiona said, twisting viciously against her bonds. "He was lying. I'm the only one who knows."

"I like a brave woman," Shevchenko said, stretching the edges of his mouth upward in an expression that had little in common with a smile. "Don't you, Mr. Hunt?" He shot a look in Fiona's direction. "I promise, my dear, you will have an opportunity to show your bravery soon enough, for what is braver than facing pain with—"

Gabriel didn't give Shevchenko time to finish his sentence. He threw the shovel as hard as he could at the dapper Ukrainian and dove to the cold stone floor, rolling swiftly behind one of the wooden pillars. He heard the shovel connect with its target, followed by another throaty exclamation from the Desert Eagle. Sharp chips of stone flew upward from the ancient floor to pepper Gabriel's shins.

"Really, Mr. Hunt," Shevchenko said, "hiding like a child. You should face your fate like a man." There was a pause, followed by a yelp of pain and a curse from Fiona. "But if you prefer to listen to the torture of Dr.

Rush first, please be my guest. You may come out whenever you are ready."

From his vantage point behind the pillar, Gabriel swiftly scanned the room. The stone stairs. The other pillars. Bare floors. The sputtering flames from the bone-tallow candles in stone bowls, supplemented by a few torches clamped into rusted metal holders. Nothing within reach that would make an adequate weapon. Djordji was bleeding out, Fiona was about to be tortured, and there didn't seem to be a damn thing Gabriel could do about it. Then he looked back at the stairs and spotted the first knife the man in the fur hat had thrown at him. It stuck out of the ground at a 45-degree angle. But it was too far away—if he went for it, he'd be shot before he made it halfway there.

"Please stop," Fiona said, her voice ragged and out of breath. "Please. I'll tell you anything." Her voice fell to a whisper Gabriel could barely hear. "Anything. Just stop."

"I will be glad to, Fiona," Shevchenko said, "provided that you tell me what I want to know."

She said something Gabriel couldn't make out.

"Speak up," Shevchenko said.

"I can't," Fiona said, a trace louder, but then her voice fell again. "I can't. But come here, I'll . . . I'll tell you where it is. It's in . . ."

There was a beat of silence and Gabriel risked a glance around the pillar just in time to see Shevchenko lean close to hear what she was saying. Fiona leaned in, caught Shevchenko's earlobe in her teeth and bit deeply. The Ukrainian let out a furious, almost feminine scream.

Gabriel ran for the stairs. Halfway across, he launched himself through the air and, coming down, slid till he fetched up against the bottom step, like a runner stealing third base. He grabbed the knife, wrenching it from the ground. He didn't let himself think about how sweaty his hands were, or how close Shevchenko was to Fiona, or what would happen to her if he missed. He just let the knife fly.

The blade flashed across the room and buried itself in the back of Shevchenko's neck. The Ukrainian spun to face Gabriel, his formerly expressionless face contorting into a horrible grimace. He tried to raise the heavy automatic in Gabriel's direction, but it tumbled from his shaking hand and he swiftly followed his gun to the stone floor.

"Christ, Gabriel," Fiona said as he got up and ran to her. "You couldn't have cut it any closer, could you? I thought for sure . . ."

Gabriel snatched up one of the blades the knife thrower had dropped when he'd fallen. He used it to slice through the bonds at her wrists.

"From now on," Gabriel said, slashing the ropes at her waist and ankles, "you don't get to be snide about my charmingly anachronistic sense of right and wrong. It's the only reason you're alive right now."

Freed from her bondage, Fiona collapsed into Gabriel's arms.

"I'm so sorry, Gabriel," she said, pressing her body against him, her lips inches from his. "Can you forgive me?"

Gabriel took her by the shoulders and pushed her back and away, his expression stern.

"I'll forgive you once the *kindjal* has been safely delivered to the Royal Museum," he said.

She wrapped her bruised arms protectively around her body. They both looked up suddenly as a loud, rhythmic pounding commenced overhead. Clearly the soldiers were trying a new technique to break down the barred door at the top of the stairs. That door had been holding back angry soldiers for over five hundred years, Gabriel thought; it would probably last at least a few more minutes. But what would they do when it fell?

"Gabriel," a hoarse voice said.

It was Djordji. Gabriel knelt beside him. The Gypsy gripped Gabriel's shirt with a bloody hand.

"You must escape," Djordji said, his voice weak. "There is secret tunnel. On right, trap door. It take you out to other side of hill. Go."

"We'll all go," Gabriel said. "Come on, Djo, get up."

"I cannot," Djordji said. "You go now."

The banging on the door above grew louder. Fiona grabbed at Gabriel's arm.

"He's right," she said, her eyes dark and serious. "We have to go now."

He turned back to Djordji. "Your wife would put some kind of curse on me if I left you here to die." He grabbed the Gypsy's good arm and hauled him up across his shoulders in a fireman's carry. Djordji made a stifled airless sound of pain but did not protest.

"Now where's this tunnel," Gabriel said. "And Fiona—don't even think of trying to give me the slip again."

"No offense, Gabriel," she said as she grabbed a torch off the wall, "but right now you're not the one I'm most worried about."

"Where's this trap door, Djordji?" Gabriel said, looking around desperately.

"You're standing on it," Djordji whispered, and looking down Gabriel could just barely make out a rectangular outline in the dirt-covered stone and a well-concealed pull-ring at its center. If he hadn't been told about it, he could've searched for hours and never noticed it.

They drew the trap door shut behind them just as the soldiers finally broke through above and started barreling down the stairs.

Inside, the tunnel was dark, damp and claustrophobic. The guttering torch provided the only light. Gabriel had to walk in a crouch to prevent Djordji from banging repeatedly into the low ceiling as he lay, stoic and bleeding, across Gabriel's shoulders. They passed broken bottles and small moldering piles of skin magazines; the flickering orange torchlight revealed a vast quantity of crude graffiti on the stone walls. There was a smell of urine and stale beer. The tunnel twisted and turned, seeming to go on forever.

"How did you know about this tunnel?" Gabriel asked, keeping his voice low.

Djordji answered in a whisper. "I played here as a boy. With other Roma—we hide from police, or just come at night to share a bottle, smoke cigarettes."

"Didn't anyone ever tell you smoking is hazardous to your health?" Gabriel said, and he felt Djordji's injured body wracked with silent laughter.

It was the better part of an hour before the air freshened and a faint gleam of moonlight became visible at the far end of the tunnel. A sudden gust of night wind killed the sputtering torch in Fiona's hand, leaving them in near total blackness. Gabriel instinctively reached out in the dark to grab Fiona's hand, to prevent her from making a run for it. He wound up with a soft handful of an entirely different body part.

"Why, Gabriel," Fiona said. "I was sure you'd lost all interest by now."

Gabriel shifted his grip to her upper arm.

"Come on," he said, as he led her toward the crooked metal doors at the far end of the tunnel.

When they reached the doors, Gabriel found them chained closed, but luckily the lock had been smashed by the latest generation of Roma teenagers. At his direction, Fiona unwrapped the chain and shoved the doors open. Gabriel gently let Djordji down off his shoulders to rest against a pile of large smooth stones. The Gypsy sighed heavily. He seemed to be doing better now that the initial shock had passed, but he was still pale and wincing with pain.

"So," Gabriel said, to Fiona. "Where is it?"

She pushed her tangled hair back off her forehead and winked, then began to unzip her dress.

"For crying out loud, what are you doing . . ."

She shucked off the dress. It pooled at her feet. Beneath it, between a filmy, transparent bra and tiny silk panties, she wore an ornate corset with gold stitching. She unfastened a compartment in the side of the thickly boned corset. To Gabriel's astonishment, the golden *kindjal* slid out of the lining. She held it up in the moonlight.

"You had it on you the whole time?" Gabriel said.

"Unlike you, Gabriel, I don't trust other people," she said. "Or hiding places I can't feel against my skin." She handed him the dagger after a moment's hesitation. Then she favored him with a slow, sultry smile. "No hard feelings, then?"

Gabriel had plenty of hard feelings at that moment, looking at her standing there with the moonlight on her pale skin, shivering slightly in the cool night breeze. He was having a tough time remembering how she'd betrayed and tried to kill him. Lucky for him, Djordji picked that moment to speak up.

"I would like hospital now, please," he said.

"Well," Fiona said, picking up her dress and wriggling back into it, "that's that, then. You should be happy, Gabriel. I know how badly you hate to lose."

She gestured for Gabriel to zip her up. When he had, she turned to face him, looking up into his eyes.

"Enjoy it while it lasts," she said. "Next time I may just end up on top." She was close enough to kiss him, but didn't. She just spun on her heel and strode away.

Gabriel reached out a hand to help Djordji up. "Think you can walk?" Gabriel said.

With a groan, Djordji heaved himself to his feet. Gabriel steadied him. "I think so."

Gabriel watched Fiona walk away across the moonlit steppe. He knew he ought to go after her, bring her in to the police of any of the three countries he'd chased her through—she'd broken no shortage of laws. But Djordji's injury was more pressing, and even if it hadn't been . . . somehow Gabriel just didn't think he could have brought himself to do it. He looked down at the *kindjal*, which Djordji was staring at like he couldn't quite believe it was real, then back up at Fiona's retreating figure. Why had she done it, he wondered. Any of it—seducing him, betraying him, handing over the *kindjal* in the end. One thing he knew: No matter how far he traveled, or how much he learned, or how many extraordinary things he witnessed, he'd never be able to understand women.

Chapter 5

Gabriel was tired, cranky and stiff by the time he arrived at the Sutton Place brownstone that housed the offices of the Hunt Foundation. His younger brother Michael had left him an urgent message to come over as soon as his plane touched down at JFK, so he'd sent his minimal baggage on to his rooms on the top floor of the Discoverers League building and told the driver to bring him directly here. When Stefan pulled the long black town car away, Gabriel stood for a moment on the steps before going inside. As was frequently the case after a particularly arduous mission, he felt a strange kind of melancholy settle in upon his return to the city of his birth. There was part of him that was glad to be home—but another part was already itching to head off again.

He had no idea how quickly he would get his wish.

Michael was, as usual, in the library, head buried in a leather-bound volume so large it threatened to topple the mahogany bookstand on which he'd precariously balanced it. His sandy hair, or what remained of it, was neatly combed, and when he looked up Gabriel saw from the dark circles under his eyes that he'd been spending too many late hours in this room and too few asleep in the apartment one floor overhead. Michael looked Gabriel up and down and opened his mouth as if about to speak. Gabriel held up one weary hand.

"Look, I don't want to hear another I told you so." Gabriel said. Michael had never liked Fiona. "You were right."

"Gabriel," Michael said. "I . . ."

"All that matters," Gabriel said, cutting his brother off as he removed his battered bomber jacket and unbuttoned the rumpled khaki work shirt he'd been wearing for nearly forty-eight hours of delayed and endlessly rescheduled travel, "is that the *kindjal* is safe at the Royal Museum where it belongs." He peeled the shirt off and twisted his stiff shoulders like a boxer warming up for a fight. "But I could sure use a long hot shower. And a cold drink."

That was when Gabriel noticed that there were two ice-filled glasses sitting on dark marble coasters on the antique cherrywood reading table. One of the glasses had a crescent of red lipstick on the rim.

"Gabriel," Michael said. "Allow me to introduce Ms. Velda Silver."

"Hello, Mr. Hunt," said a warm, silken voice behind him.

Gabriel turned to face a tall, auburn-haired beauty. She sized up his shirtless chest with an arched eyebrow and a look of amusement in her wide-set hazel eyes. She looked to be in her middle twenties, conservatively dressed in a dark suit and simple heels, but the body beneath the drab professional exterior was anything but drab. Strong and athletic yet still distinctly feminine, with a generous, natural bust and graceful, rounded hips. She seemed way too tan and healthy to be a native New Yorker—but then so did Gabriel. She looked, he thought, like the kind of woman who held down an executive position during the week but went white-water rafting or mountain climbing when Saturday came around. Her legs in particular were breathtaking.

Gabriel casually tossed his shirt over the back of a chair as if he routinely greeted guests bare-chested, smiled and extended his hand to her.

"What can I do for you, Ms. Silver?" he asked.

She took Gabriel's hand with a warm, strong grip. Her nails were short and unpainted. Her gaze, a challenge.

"I have a proposal for you," she replied. "I'm organizing an important expedition and I'd very much like to have you head it up."

Gabriel looked over at Michael, whose expression told Gabriel that he had already heard her pitch and thought the woman was off her rocker. Gabriel shrugged.

"Okay, shoot," he said.

"My father," she said, "Dr. Lawrence Silver, has been working for seven years at a remote research station near the South Pole, studying the effects of global warming. I've visited him there twice, the last time just six months ago. Things seemed to be going fine. Then a few days ago I got word that he disappeared during a routine trip to sample core ice from the site of an unusual formation. He's been missing for over two weeks."

Gabriel looked at Michael again and then back at Velda. Even during what passed for summer at the South Pole, two weeks lost without food or shelter was as good as dead.

"I'm very sorry to hear that, Ms. Silver," Gabriel said. "But I'm no expert in polar search and rescue. If

I'm known for anything, it's finding lost artifacts, not lost people."

"I'm well aware of your field of expertise," Velda said. "That's why I came to you. Every reasonable rescue effort to save my father has already been made by a highly qualified search and rescue team. Tragically, to no avail." She paused, pressed her lips into a tight, anxious line. "But there's more. May I have another drink, please?"

Michael refilled her glass from a crystal decanter of fifteen-year-old single malt scotch and then poured a glass for Gabriel as well.

"Thank you," she said, taking a sip of the scotch and then sucking a small piece of ice between her even white teeth. "I think my father found something truly extraordinary before he lost contact with the research station. You are one of the few people in the world I believe would be open-minded enough to help me track it down and comprehend it. I have a recording of my father's last transmission. Would you be willing to listen to it?"

"Sure," Gabriel said, downing a healthy swallow of his scotch.

Velda took a CD in an unmarked jewel case from her purse and handed it to Michael, who slipped it into the laptop computer sitting on the far side of the reading table.

After a few seconds of silence, broken only by the tapping of Michael's efficient keystrokes, a harsh cloud of static came out of the computer's speaker, followed by a male voice, struggling to be heard over the background noise.

"... *a deep, vertical fissure* ..." The voice faded in and out; only disjointed fragments of sentences came through. "*I am uninjured but unable to* ..." A burst of static drowned out what he was unable to do. ". . . *suddenly quite warm . . .*"

There was a lengthy pause, nothing but a low soft hiss punctuated by occasional pops and crackles.

"I don't—" Gabriel started to say.

"Sh," Velda said. "Listen." Then to Michael: "Could you please turn up the volume?"

More hissing, only louder now. Gabriel was starting to suspect Michael was right about Velda; the Foundation certainly got its share of crazies, mostly by mail (or these days, e-mail), but once in a while showing up in person. Of course, most of them didn't look as appealing as this one, but—

As he was about to politely send her on her way, the male voice spoke again, a single distinct sentence rising above the ambient noise.

"*I see . . . trees,*" the incredulous voice said.

Then the recording abruptly ended, leaving the room hushed and its occupants thoughtful and silent.

"Trees?" Gabriel repeated. "There are no trees in Antarctica."

"Precisely," Velda said. "I think my father stumbled upon some kind of climatic anomaly. A hidden, subterranean warm spot—perhaps a preserved window into Antarctica's verdant prehistoric past. Furthermore, in an environment where trees could survive, it might be possible for my father to survive as well, for longer than normal, anyway. Mr. Hunt, I believe that my father could still be alive. I believe that he has discovered something of unprecedented scientific and historical significance, and I want to organize an immediate expedition to trace his path, verify his findings . . . and hopefully bring him home alive." Her cheeks were flushed, her eyes bright. "Are you with me, Mr. Hunt?"

Gabriel had to admit he was intrigued. He emptied his glass and set it down.

"Let me make some calls," Gabriel said. "I'll get back to you in two hours with a definite answer."

Velda nodded and tossed back the rest of her drink.

"Thank you, Mr. Hunt," she said, setting a simple off-white business card on the table alongside her now empty glass. "I look forward to your response."

Gabriel couldn't help watching the graceful sway of her hips and tan, muscular legs as she walked swiftly away.

"What do you make of that?" Gabriel asked his brother, once she was gone.

"Lawrence Silver is seventy-five years old," Michael said. "He's a tough specimen—survived one of the camps as a child; Buchenwald, I think—but still, seventy-five is no age to be traipsing around the South Pole. Then this . . ." Michael shook his head. "The poor man was obviously near death and hallucinating at the time he made that transmission. Modern geothermal imaging and satellite photography have mapped every inch of the Antarctic landscape. No 'warm spot' could possibly exist and escape detection." He pressed the Eject key and Velda Silver's CD slid out of the computer. He tossed it on a stack of rejected grant proposals. "You would have to be as deluded as she obviously is to take on a pointless and dangerous expedition like this."

Gabriel nodded, taking his shirt off the back of the chair.

"That's what I figured you'd say." Gabriel slid his arms back into the shirtsleeves. "How would you fly into Antarctica anyway? Christchurch to McMurdo, and then inland from there?"

"For heaven's sake, Gabriel," Michael said. "Surely you're not considering—"

Gabriel buttoned his shirt and grabbed his jacket. "Considering it? Of course I'm not considering it," Gabriel said, and Michael sighed with relief. It was short-lived.

"I've decided," Gabriel said.

Chapter 6

The Christchurch pub where Gabriel had arranged to meet the other members of the expedition was—prophetically?—called the Hot Spot and had a jaunty hellfire theme featuring buxom cartoon devil girls and lurid flames on the black walls. The clientele was about a third Kiwi locals and two-thirds Antarctic researchers and McMurdo support staff, either on the way in or on the way out. The ones on the way in were quiet and thoughtful, savoring their last Guinness on tap while working up the nerve to face the killing cold, darkness and isolation of the coming Antarctic winter. The ones on the way out were scruffy, unkempt and pale as the ice they'd just left behind, except for masks of peeling pink sunburn that outlined the shape of now-absent goggles. They were also, without exception, falling-down drunk.

When Gabriel entered, he could see the pub's inhabitants trying to size him up, attempting to fit him into one of the three categories and failing. He was searching through the curious, occasionally hostile faces, looking for his people, when he overheard the tail end of a loud conversation about a Harley chopper the guy talking had had extensively customized by some celebrity mechanic with his own TV show and air-shipped over from the States. The proud owner was going on and on about all the special expensive features of his brand-new toy and Gabriel smiled slightly to himself. If Rue Aparecido was anywhere within earshot, there would be no way she'd be able to keep out of that conversation.

Sure enough, just as Gabriel spotted the heavily tattooed Kiwi biker who was boasting loudly about his recent acquisition, he heard Rue's distinct, husky Brazilian accent cut right through the bar noise and chatter.

"Might as well put a saddle on your ninety-year-old grandma and ride her around," Rue said. "She'd be faster, handle better and be less likely to die under your ass."

The biker turned and Gabriel followed his gaze to where Rue stood alone against the bar. She was in her early twenties, whippet-thin and wiry with close-cropped dark hair, sharp black-coffee eyes and two hundred pounds of attitude packed into her hundred-pound body. The youngest child of a family of ten, she was the only daughter, an unapologetic tomboy with engine grease under her fingernails and utter disdain for anything she saw as frivolous or girly, such as makeup or high heels. Rue was a crackerjack mechanic in love with all things vehicular. Anything that flew, floated or submerged, she could pilot. Anything with wheels, she could drive. And if it broke down, she could fix it with nothing but elbow-grease and sweet talk.

Gabriel grinned in recognition when he saw her. Rue had a heavy sweatshirt tied by the sleeves around her waist. Even in the loose-fitting cargo pants she favored, there was no hiding the one part of her otherwise boy-ish body that was unabashedly feminine: her round, curvy backside. She'd always been self-conscious about it and habitually tied long-sleeved shirts around her waist to cover it up. Gabriel wasn't fooled. He'd seen that particular feature up close and personal, without all the layers of tomboy camouflage. It was more than a year ago now, but he still felt a kind of melancholy ache under his sternum when he thought about the time they'd spent together. Today was the first time he'd seen Rue since she'd told him, over a crackling phone line, that long-distance relationships were not something she did, not even for him, and gave him a choice: move in or move on. He'd made the only choice he could, and she'd accepted it and moved on too, with no bad feelings and no looking back. It hadn't been quite so easy for Gabriel. He'd been of two minds about asking her to join this expedition, but she was the only person he knew who had practical Antarctic experience. She'd done a few summers as a mechanic in the Heavy Shop at McMurdo Station and knew people on the ice who would be able to get them inland with minimal bureaucratic interfer-ence. It made all the sense in the world to involve her—but that didn't make seeing her again any easier.

"What the hell do you know about it?" the biker asked Rue, fixing her with his beery, bloodshot gaze.

"A hell of a lot more than you, apparently," Rue re-plied, taking a swig of her Tui Brew 5 and wiping the foam from her upper lip with her knuckles. "I know well enough not to get my bank account cleaned out by a gang of celebrity *babacas* who think it's perfectly acceptable to bend and force their goofy custom parts to fit the frame because they were too stupid to factor in the extra eighth of an inch before powder-coating."

"Oh yeah," the biker said, flushing a deep, dangerous crimson. "Let's see your ride, then."

"I've got a beat-up 99 Suzuki Hayabusa that I'm working on back home in Sao Paulo," she said with a shrug. "She'll do 300 kilometers per hour without breaking a sweat, but she doesn't have bat wings or neon, or a football helmet welded to the frame, so I guess I have no idea what makes a real bad-ass ride. On the other hand, I could race your Malibu Barbie Dream Chopper on roller skates and still leave you in the dust."

"Well why don't you then?" the biker asked, taking a threatening step toward Rue, big hands clenching. "Right now, if you think you're so goddamn clever."

"I'd love to," she said with a smirk. "But I can't stand to see a grown man cry."

"Why, if you were a bloke, I'd . . ."

"You'd what?" Gabriel asked, stepping swiftly in between Rue and the biker.

"And who the fuck are you?" the biker asked. "Her bodyguard?"

"Nah," replied Millie Ventrose, rising suddenly out of the crowd like the calm eye of a storm. "That'd be me."

Maximillian Ventrose, Jr., Millie to his friends, was the second team member Gabriel had come here to meet. Three hundred pounds of solid muscle with twelve-inch fists and a boxer's profile under his faded Saints cap, he stood six foot seven barefoot and looked like he could wrestle an alligator one handed without spilling his coffee. But there was a profound, Zen-like calm about him that ran contrary to his thuggish features and massive physique. He'd grown up in Chalmette, Louisiana, just southeast of New Orleans, and his deep, soft voice with its odd, almost Brooklynesque Yat accent possessed a mysterious power to smooth over even the most heated disagreements. Of course, anyone drunk, cranked or foolish enough to resist the calming power of Millie's warm molasses voice was swiftly made to change his mind about fighting through more direct means. Usually by way of the local emergency room.

"That your chopper out front?" Millie asked.

"Yeah," the biker replied. "You got something to say about it too?"

"That a Baker right-hand drive six-speed trans you got on there?" Millie asked.

"Hell, yeah," the biker replied. "Gives her better balance with the fat tires. 'Course it costs twice as much as the standard left-hand drive, but I wouldn't have it any other way."

"Really?" Millie asked, nodding thoughtfully and stepping to one side, subtly pulling the biker's focus away from Rue. "Ain't that somethin'."

Less than a minute later, Millie had the biker right back on track, jawing about his precious motorcycle as if Rue's interjection had never happened.

"Gabriel," Velda called, turning every head in the bar as she walked across the room. Even in her simple tweed skirt and high-necked blouse, it was impossible not to stare. "There you are. I apologize for being late."

"It's all right," Gabriel replied. "I just got here a minute ago myself." As she reached his side, Velda put her arms around him and kissed his cheek. It had been a long trip over, and they'd ended it more intimate than they'd begun.

Gabriel cast a sidelong glance over Velda's shoulder at Rue, thinking perhaps he'd see some hint of jealousy. Rue gave him a bemused smirk as if she knew exactly what he was fishing for and was having none of it.

"Rue, this is Velda Silver. Velda—"

"Rue Aparecido," Rue said, extending a hand. "Mechanic, pilot, and if I'm not too far off the mark, your predecessor in the Hunt Foundation's mile-high club."

Velda stared at Rue's hand and only reached out to grasp it after an uncomfortable second or two. She said, icily, "You and Gabriel . . . ?"

"Oh, yeah," Rue said, either oblivious to the other woman's tone or deliberately ignoring it. "Like rabbits. For a couple of months. But this was a while ago. Good times, right?" She threw a light jab at Gabriel's shoulder.

"Excuse me," Gabriel said. He stepped away to pull Millie out of his conversation with his new biker buddy. One rib-cracking bear hug later, Gabriel led the big man back to meet Velda. As they came up behind her, Gabriel heard Velda asking Rue, in a voice that hadn't thawed at all, "So, tell me, has he slept with *everyone* on the team?"

"Not Millie," Rue said, grinning naughtily.

"Oh? And how did she manage to resist his charms?" Velda said.

Rue shrugged, her expression all innocence.

"Velda," Gabriel said, and she turned to face him, only the faintest of blushes darkening her cheeks at having been overheard. "I'd like to introduce you to Millie

Ventrose." And as Velda stared, puzzled, at the giant and not at all feminine torso before her: "It's short for Maximillian."

"My father's brother's called Max," Millie said, "for Maxwell. So Millie's what they called me. It kinda stuck."

"I see," Velda said. She glanced back over her shoulder at Rue, who grinned away the daggers being sent in her direction. "It is a pleasure to meet you . . . Millie."

"Maybe we should get down to business," Gabriel said.

"Yes," Velda said. "Let's."

Gabriel found them an empty table and scavenged an extra chair from the next table over. He'd already briefed Rue and Millie by phone on the general details of the expedition, but Velda took the next fifteen minutes to fill in all the blanks. When she spoke about the possibilities of what her father might have discovered, her frigid tone finally vanished and her eyes filled with a bright childlike hope and excitement.

"I have made the arrangements for us to fly out to McMurdo in three hours," Velda said. "All the severe-weather clothing and equipment we will need for the expedition will be coming with us on the plane. For now, I suggest that we return to our respective hotels to change and make any other final arrangements, and then meet at the airfield at seven thirty. Agreed?"

"Agreed," Gabriel said. "On one condition." He looked from Velda to Rue and back again. "The two of you aren't going to have a problem getting along, are you? I'm serious. When we're out there on the ice, there can't be any distractions, any fights, any squabbling, any anything. Understood?"

"You know you can count on me," Rue said.

"I do know that," Gabriel said. "Velda . . . ?"

"Let's not forget," she said, "it's my father's life we're talking about. I don't think any of you could possibly be more serious than I am."

"All right then," Gabriel said, slapping Millie's broad shoulder. "Let's do it."

Chapter 7

Gabriel looked out the military plane's tiny round window as the twinkling lights of Christchurch receded beneath scattered cloud cover. Millie slept with his massive arms crossed and his Saints cap pulled down over his eyes. Velda looked calm and gorgeous, dressed as if ready to shoot a Ralph Lauren ad in Aspen. Only her hands betrayed the anxiety she felt, clenching and unclenching and periodically smoothing her pristine and wrinkle-free trousers. Rue sat directly across from Gabriel, chewing a piece of gum and cleaning the engine oil from under her fingernails with a plastic swizzle stick bearing the logo of the airport bar.

"Ever been to Mactown before?" Rue asked.

"Where?" Gabriel looked away from the window, which now afforded a dull flat view of dark water stretching out forever in every direction.

"McMurdo Station," Rue said. "You know, the place we're going."

Gabriel shook his head. "I've been to the North Pole, but never to Antarctica."

"Well, imagine that," Rue teased, her dark eyes bright. "This poor little *paulista* has been somewhere

that the brave adventurer Gabriel Hunt has yet to con-
quer." She kicked Gabriel's boot with her toe.

"I'm sure it's an amazing place," Gabriel said, looking back out into the darkness. "So much grim, bloody
history. The stark, pristine beauty of untouched glaciers. The struggle to triumph over the brutal elements
in the last real uncharted wilderness left on earth."

"Right," Rue said with an arched eyebrow. "Better
get some sleep. You're going to have more stark, pristine beauty than you know what to do with—twenty-
four hours a day of it. Remember, the sun never sets
during the Antarctic summer, so . . ."

"So this will be our last dark night," Gabriel said.

"Pretty much," Rue said.

He flicked off the overhead light, closed his eyes and
slept.

"So," Rue said. "What do you say? Is this pristine
beauty or what?"

The four of them sat on orange plastic chairs that
would not have looked out of place at New York City's
DMV waiting room in 1972. At the far end of the room
was a scarred metal desk with nothing on it. The walls
were cheap wood paneling and the only decoration was
a pair of faded posters, one featuring cute penguins and
the other cute seals. Besides a couple of seagulls, this
was the only wildlife they'd seen in the eighteen hours
since they'd landed at McMurdo airport.

"Christ," Millie said, shifting his long legs awkwardly in front of his tiny seat. "I feel like I'm in trouble with the sisters back in grade school."

Outside the charmless metal building, the temperature
hovered at 22 degrees below zero, but inside it was

uncomfortably stuffy and overheated. The accumulated snow in their boot treads had rapidly melted into dirty puddles around their feet. In spite of the gurgling, spitting humidifier in one corner of the room, the air was so dry Gabriel could almost feel his lips chapping as they waited. Several attempts to contact Michael on the expensive satellite phone he'd insisted Gabriel bring had resulted in frustrating fifteen-second bursts of asking each other "Can you hear me?" followed by the inevitable loss of signal.

Before Gabriel could come up with a good answer to Rue's question, a new bureaucrat entered the room. This one was female, but otherwise virtually identical to the two that had spoken to them before. Her sour, constipated expression did not bode well for the expedition.

"I'm Celia Lanke. Executive DP here at McMurdo. Mr. . . ." She looked down at a plastic clipboard and then back up at Gabriel, her gaze baleful. "Hunt. You claim that you've already filed your 679-A, but I'm afraid Denver has not been able to confirm that any such filing actually occurred. Because of the urgency of your stated mission, I have requested and received the go-ahead to allow you to refile, but there will be a refiling fee of thirty-five dollars."

"That's fine," Gabriel said.

"Let me finish. Expedited processing can still take up to ten business days and there will be an additional priority processing fee of two hundred dollars. You will also be charged an assessment of fifty dollars per person for room and board while you wait; however, with Offload only two weeks away, we are currently at full boarding capacity. It will be up to you to organize your own sleeping accommodations as best you can."

She clicked a ballpoint pen and handed the clipboard to Gabriel. "The NSF cannot be expected to babysit private parties, nor can we allow any interference with the scientific research being conducted in our facilities. Any violation of the visitor code of conduct listed on page 27C will result in immediate expulsion of your entire party on the next plane to Christchurch, at your own expense."

"The expenses are no problem," Gabriel said. "I'd gladly pay more if it would help. What is a problem is the ten-day delay. Is there any way—"

"Mr. Hunt," the woman said. "I don't make the rules, and they don't let me change them either. Just because you've got money doesn't mean you rule the roost—not down here. The fees are what they are and so is the wait. If you don't like it, you can take the next plane out. Do we understand each other?"

She left without waiting for a response. Gabriel looked down at the clipboard. The stack of forms to be filled out was over an inch thick.

"Ten days!" Velda said.

A young man in filthy brown coveralls chose that moment to slip in through the back door of the room. He had a big smile and long, wild hair and a six-pack of cheap beer in one hand. He stank of diesel fuel so powerfully it made Gabriel's head swim.

"Hey, Ruda!" the man cried, pulling Rue into an embrace that lifted her off her feet. "I heard you were back on the ice, but I couldn't believe it."

"I can't believe it either," Rue said, smiling at Gabriel over the young man's shoulder.

"Strip Monopoly just isn't the same without you. You planning to winter-over?"

"No chance, Dusty," Rue replied, taking a beer and

cracking it open. "Six months with you and Tanner in the dark and I'd be ready to chew my own leg off. I'm just here to help a friend. In and out."

"Well, that's the way to help a friend all right," Dusty said, nudging her with an elbow. He began passing the remaining beers around, shaking everyone's hand as he went. Only Velda declined the beer. Dusty held his can up in a toast. "Skal!"

"Skal," Gabriel said. Gabriel wasn't normally much of a beer drinker—but the way this one went down his parched, bone-dry throat, it tasted like the best he'd ever had.

"Skal," Rue repeated, sucking foam from the mouth of the can. "Is Speedo still doing Pole run?"

"Of course," Dusty said. "In fact, he's got one in about forty minutes, why?"

Rue pulled a twenty-ounce plastic bottle of Moxie soda pop from the messenger bag she wore slung over one hip and passed it to Dusty.

"Ah, you do love me after all," Dusty said with a huge grin, clutching the bottle to his heart as if it were a teddy bear. "A winter without Moxitinis is like a fat girl with itty bitty titties."

"I think now would be a good time to file that harassment complaint against Tanner," Rue said. "Don't you?"

"Oh, yes," Dusty said. "High time."

"Just make sure it keeps Lanke occupied for at least, oh, forty minutes?"

"Not a problem," Dusty said, slipping the bottle into one of the many enormous pockets on his coverall and downing the rest of his beer in one long gulp. "Good luck out there, Ruda." He headed out toward Lanke's office.

Rue smiled over at Velda. "Those ten days just flew by, didn't they?"

Bundled up in extreme weather gear and lugging their equipment like a line of ants at the world's coldest picnic, Gabriel and the team made their way through icy winds down a narrow runway of smooth snow toward a growling ski-equipped LC-130.

The pilot—Speedo—turned out to be a handsome, weathered sort with merry blue eyes and a troublemaker's grin. He was clearly thrilled to be breaking the rules. He helped the team unload three pallets of frozen Tater Tots to make room for their gear and did so with all the glee of a teenager preparing to sneak out after curfew. According to Rue, Speedo had some shadowy, possibly sexual ties to a prominent female senator, and was therefore un-fireable and able to get away with murder up here.

"So," Millie asked the pilot as they worked together to secure the gear for takeoff. "Why do they call you Speedo?"

"What do you think?" he replied, heading for the cockpit. "I'm the fastest you'll ever see. Maybe you'd better buckle up, son."

After he closed the cockpit door, Rue said, "Fast's got nothing to do with it. I bet him once he wouldn't run from the Heavy Shop to Crary Lab and back in nothing but bunny boots and his little bathing suit," she said. "He won the bet. Everyone calls him Speedo ever since."

"So he isn't fast?" Millie said.

"I didn't say that," Rue said.

The ride to the Pole was choppy and uncomfortable but otherwise uneventful, giving Gabriel and his team time to gawk out the windows at the awe-inspiring landscape below. It was 10:30 P.M. but the sun shone bright as noon across the towering blue glaciers and curious, surreal formations of windblown ice. At first they saw fat seals huddled together in writhing brown masses the size of football fields and large troops of penguins clustered around the edges of slushy holes in the endless frozen sea, but as they moved inexorably southward, deeper into the cold dead interior of the continent, living things became more scarce and eventually vanished altogether. The plane flew low over soaring white mountain ranges like giant carnivorous teeth and grim, dead valleys with no ice at all, just scattered stone and dry, barren dirt. Eventually the landscape flattened out to an endless stretch of frozen nothing. When they finally spotted the distinctive geodesic dome of Amundsen-Scott South Pole Station, Gabriel felt Velda grip his gloved hand, her long thigh pressing against his as she leaned closer to the window.

Speedo put the big cargo plane down on the ice with a bone-jarring bump and rattle. Velda's hold on Gabriel's hand tightened, then released.

When Gabriel exited the plane, he was not prepared for the raw and brutal power of the wind. It leapt on him like a hungry tiger, tearing at his exposed face and nearly knocking him flat. He had heard that the South Pole was the windiest place on earth, but knowing it and experiencing it were two totally different things.

On the long, frozen airstrip, the team was met by what appeared to be an enormous Yeti. He was taller than Millie, with a long, ice-encrusted yellow beard and featureless black goggles sticking out of the fur hood of a safety-orange parka.

"Velda," the Yeti cried in a heavy Scandinavian accent. Gabriel had to strain to hear over the roar of the engines and the howling wind. "We did not know if you would make it."

"Nils," Velda shouted back. "It's good to see you. How is Elaine?"

"She is well." Nils turned to Millie. "This must be Gabriel Hunt."

Millie smiled and shook his head.

"Millie Ventrose," he said, shaking the Yeti's gloved hand. "That's Gabriel."

The Yeti looked over and down. At six feet even, Gabriel rarely felt small, but standing between these two mountains could give any man outside the NBA a complex.

"Pleased to meet you, Nils," Gabriel said, sticking out a hand.

When Nils took it to shake, Gabriel felt something odd and unbalanced in the other man's grip. It took him a minute to realize that the last two fingers of the man's glove were empty.

"This is Rue Aparecido," Gabriel said, just to have something to say.

"Oh, we know Rue here," Nils said. "We know her *very* well."

Rue blew the Yeti a jaunty kiss and went to start unloading their gear.

So, tell me, Gabriel was suddenly tempted to ask, *has she slept with* everyone *on the team?* But he kept the thought to himself.

"Nils Engen worked with my father at the ComNet research station," Velda said, leaning close but still shouting to be heard. "He's been on the ice for fifteen years, ten of them at or near Pole. He's agreed to be our guide."

"Good," Gabriel said, grabbing his pack and slinging it up on his shoulder. "Glad to have you, Nils."

When they had all gathered their gear and bid Speedo their hollered good-byes, Nils led them past the edge of the dome to a battered Spryte snowcat that looked like a rusty orange shoe box on wide tank treads. The driver was a grim woman in a gray parka that Nils introduced as Skua. She didn't speak a word for their entire journey.

The Spryte was turtle slow, had no real suspension of any kind and was both horrifically noisy and foul smelling, belching plumes of toxic exhaust that wafted back into the badly insulated cab. The tiny, slotlike side windows quickly iced up, making them pretty much useless. The ice over which they traveled was scored with windblown ridges that bounced and rattled their frozen bones. Millie hit his head against the roof so many times he wondered loud if he shouldn't have worn a helmet.

Their first view of the research station out the front windshield made it look like a beer can lying discarded and half buried on the featureless ice of the vast Polar Plateau. The only other visible landmark was the distant hump of Pole Station to the east. No mountains, no glaciers, nothing for the eye to focus on but miles and miles of flat white below and flat blue above. The altitude made breathing feel like doing push-ups. The bone-dry wind that came whistling in was even more vicious, full of knives and the promise of frostbite, hypothermia and death. The vast emptiness made Gabriel feel small and fragile, and he thought even men like Nils and Millie must find it humbling.

"Velda!" a tiny, plump figure cried, appearing in the doorway of the beer can as the snowcat slowly ground to a halt. Any human features were buried under layers of down and goggles, but the voice sounded female. "It's so good to see you!"

"Elaine," Velda said, stepping forward to embrace the shorter woman. "How are you managing out here?"

"We're doing okay," she replied. "We were supposed to get a new fish in to winter-over, but I guess he failed his pych eval, so it'll just be the three of us this year." She paused, then gripped Velda's gloved hand. "I'm so sorry about your father."

There was a long windy minute of awkward silence. The cold was rapidly becoming excruciating, a sensation more of pain than of temperature.

"You idiots are welcome to say out here sunbathing," Skua said, piping up for the first time. "I'm going in."

"Come on," Elaine said. "Let's get you kids warmed up."

Chapter 8

The inside of the tiny research station looked and smelled like a college dorm. In the main living area there was a random scattering of cheap, questionable furniture. Cartoons and sketches and photos torn from magazines were thumbtacked to the walls. A green lava lamp stood next to a big-screen TV that was hooked up to an Xbox. A heavy funk of armpits and fried food hung in the air alongside a lingering hint of marijuana smoke. Skua had swiftly retired to unseen private quarters, but with the six of them standing there, the narrow room felt like a rush-hour subway car. Taking their parkas off was a major challenge in the cramped space, all awkward elbows and bumping into one another. Millie could barely move without sticking his elbow in someone's face or cracking his head against one of the metal spines supporting the roof. There was one small couch and a sad, broken-down recliner, meaning even if three of them squeezed onto the couch, two people would still have nowhere to sit. The low curved ceiling just added to the claustrophobia. Gabriel couldn't imagine living like this for months at a time, especially during the sunless winter, when spending time outside was even less of an option.

Once out of her gear, Elaine revealed herself to be a plump, light-skinned black woman in her early fifties with dreadlocked white hair and a scattering of dark freckles across her round face. Stripped of his bulky down, Nils was less of a Yeti than a gangly stork. His blond thinning hair was pulled back into a wispy ponytail and the goggles were replaced by round, wire-rimmed glasses. He was missing two-thirds of his right ring finger and all of the pinkie. Even though the big Swede had to be close to seven feet tall, he seemed entirely comfortable with the low ceiling, crouching instinctively and gracefully as he moved through the cramped space.

"I'll mix us up some hot chocolate," Elaine said. "Nils, why don't you bring in a couple more chairs from the mess hall?"

The two researchers left the room and Gabriel sat down in the recliner, wondering if this whole expedition really had been a mistake after all. He looked over at Velda, who was standing at the far end of the room with her arms wrapped around herself, her hazel eyes distant. Maybe Michael had been right. He wasn't always, but he did have a good nose for futility.

When Nils returned with a spindly folding chair under each arm, he motioned for Gabriel to stand.

"It's Elaine's week for the recliner," Nils said apologetically, handing a folding chair out to Gabriel. "We rotate on a weekly basis so that everyone is allowed fair and equal usage. Short-term visitors are not included." He pointed to a hand-drawn chart on the wall labeled RECLINER SCHEDULE. "You may laugh, but we need these kinds of rules out here. It's the only way to winter-over without murdering each other."

Gabriel took the folding chair and looked over at the

schedule. He couldn't help but notice that Dr. Silver's name—LAWRENCE—was X'd off each time it appeared. His recliner dates had been redistributed among the other researchers. Gabriel wondered if Velda had noticed this and was struck with an urge to comfort her. But although she stood within arm's reach, she seemed a thousand miles away.

"Well," Elaine said, reappearing with six mismatched cups on a plastic tray. "Anyone up for midrats?"

"I could eat," Nils replied, handing the other folding chair to Millie.

"Midrats?" Millie repeated, and handed the chair off to Velda. There was no way it would support his weight.

"Midnight rations," Rue explained. "With the shifts up here, there's four meals a day: breakfast, lunch, dinner and midrats."

"Well, then, yes, ma'am," Millie said. "I'd sure love a bite."

Elaine handed around the cocoa and then took her own mug and the tray back into the unseen galley. Gabriel could hear the beep and whir of a microwave. He shuddered, remembering all the boxes of Tater Tots they had unloaded from Speedo's plane, but he was hungry and in no position to be finicky.

"We'll eat and then get a few hours of sleep," Gabriel said. "How far away is the site where Dr. Silver was last seen?"

"About three hours in the Spryte," Nils replied, blowing over the rim of his steaming mug before taking a sip. "We should plan to spend no more than four hours at a stretch before returning to base camp, but we must also bring overnight supplies and tents in case we are caught out in bad weather. The reports are all clear for the next forty-eight but you never know for sure. Better to be prepared than dead."

"Story of my life," Gabriel said.

Elaine returned, the tray loaded with microwave burritos on plastic plates. She handed the plates around. "Eat up," she said. "Won't stay warm for long."

Gabriel wolfed down the food. He'd eaten worse. Of course, he'd survived for a week once in the Peruvian jungle on a diet of rainwater and grubs, so that wasn't saying much.

"I don't know about you all," Elaine said, "but I'm gonna hit the sack. Nils'll be up for another few hours working in the lab if you need anything but otherwise, you're free to bed down wherever you can find the space."

Nils began gathering up the dirty plates. "Velda," he said. "You can sleep in your father's bed, if you don't mind bunking in my room."

"That'll be fine," Velda said. Her face was closed off and unreadable.

"Rue, why don't you take the couch," Gabriel said, putting a hand on Millie's massive shoulder. "You and me are on the floor."

"I don't think there's enough floor for the two of us," Millie replied, unrolling an extra-large sleeping bag. "You know I love you like a brother, but I don't particularly want to snuggle."

"That's fine," Gabriel said. "I'll bed down in the mess hall."

Gabriel collected his bedroll and headed down a short hallway to the mess. It was barely big enough for the square card table at its center. Gabriel had to fold up the table and lean it against the wall to make room to lie down on the floor.

Once he'd done so, Gabriel discovered that he still felt wide-awake, mind restless and full of unanswered questions. After a few minutes of staring at the ceiling, he decided a hot shower would help him relax.

The first door he opened led to a cramped laboratory. It was meat-locker cold and the floor was raw exposed ice. A variety of probes had been sunk deep into the ice and twinkling banks of high-tech machines and top-of-the-line computers compiled, sorted and analyzed the data. Nils sat on a crooked stool in front of a bank of monitors. He wore a thick sweater, muffler and wool watch cap but no parka. His gloves had the tips of the fingers snipped off for easier typing and the pinkie of the right glove had been removed altogether. Although Gabriel was shivering, Nils seemed comfortable in the chill.

Nils was holding a second cup of steaming cocoa in one hand and a silver hip flask in the other. When he looked up and saw Gabriel, he finished pouring a slug of whatever the flask contained into the cocoa and then held the flask out to Gabriel. It proved to be surprisingly excellent bourbon. Gabriel took a swig and gave the flask back to the big Swede.

"Tell me," Gabriel said. "What do you make of Dr. Silver's last transmission?"

Nils took a sip of his cocoa, watching the continuous parade of numbers across the screen beside him.

"I was the one who received the transmission," he finally said. "I tried to respond but there was no reply." He paused, tapping away at the keyboard for several seconds, his face stoic. "What he claims to have seen is not possible. I believe he is dead." His expression softened slightly and he looked down into his mug. "Don't get me wrong—the man was as capable a scientist as anyone I've known, and physically? He was in better shape than most men half his age. Stronger, too." He shook his head. "But it doesn't matter how strong you are down here. The ice is stronger."

Gabriel nodded.

"I understand this is difficult for Velda. I hope seeing the place where he disappeared and confirming that his remains cannot be found, she will be able to let go and finally accept the loss."

Gabriel nodded, wrapping his arms around his body and stamping his chilly feet.

"I thought I'd take a shower," he said.

"Down at the other end of the hall," Nils said, without looking away from his monitors.

"Thanks," Gabriel said and left the big Swede to his ice and his numbers.

The other end of the dim hallway terminated in two identical doors. No way to know which was the bathroom, so he picked one at random and knocked gently.

"Yes?"

Velda's voice.

Gabriel pushed open the door to reveal a tiny dorm-like room. Two narrow beds and not much else. Twin footlockers, a small halogen reading lamp burning on one of them. Velda sat on one of the beds, her long legs drawn up beneath her chin like an anxious child. She wasn't crying, but there had been a flash of vulnerability in her face that quickly submerged when she saw Gabriel enter the room. She unfolded her legs and stood to meet him. Her thick, auburn hair was down around her face

"I was just looking for the . . ." Gabriel began, hand motioning pointlessly in the direction of the door, but she cut him off.

"Come here," she said.

She reached out to pull Gabriel into an embrace. Her lips were just inches from his, barely parted and begging for a kiss. Who was he to argue? He gave her what she wanted and she gave it back in spades, her fierce, urgent heat threatening to melt through the polar ice beneath them.

After, they lay entwined and spent in a tangle of blankets, sharing a warm, comfortable silence. Gabriel found himself drifting just on the edge of sleep when Velda spoke, almost too soft to hear.

"I have to know," Velda said. "I can't stand not knowing."

"I understand," Gabriel replied, reaching down to brush her hair back off her forehead.

He did, too. His own parents had vanished, not in the frozen Antarctic but in the heat of the Mediterranean. They'd been on a speaking tour at the end of 1999 (the theme had been prophecies surrounding the turn of the millennium) when the ship they were traveling on had vanished for three days. When it had appeared again, not a living soul had been on board, just three crew members with their throats cut. Gabriel remembered all too clearly the ache of waiting for news, of not knowing. Every time a body washed up and was identified as one of the other passengers, Gabriel was torn between feeling relieved and feeling resentful that others were being set free to mourn while he and Michael and their sister, Lucy, remained in the purgatory of not knowing. It was a terrible thing to lose hope, but terrible, too, to have it—to carry the burden of hope from day to day, watching as the odds grew slimmer, but being denied the respite of their ever dropping to zero.

In the end, the bodies of Ambrose and Cordelia Hunt had never been found. The U.S. government had declared them dead, a verdict Gabriel had reluctantly accepted—he'd certainly never been able to turn up any evidence to the contrary, and he'd tried. But acceptance wasn't the same as closure. He understood why Velda wanted closure.

"I begged him to come home," she said. "When I was here last, six months ago—I told him, Papa, you're seventy-five years old, you gave up teaching ten years ago, why can't you stop and come home? But he said no. 'Now more than ever, with global warming . . .'" She threw up her hands. "He felt his expertise was needed. He said he'd never be able to live with himself if he left the problem to others."

"Maybe he was right," Gabriel said.

"But now he's vanished," Velda said, "and all his expertise with him." She turned to Gabriel. "It's more than just not knowing if he's alive or dead. I can't help thinking that my father may have made the discovery of a lifetime. Even if . . ." Her voice caught, and she stared up at the low ceiling, collecting herself. "Even if he didn't make it," she said, finally, her voice steady and controlled, "I feel like the world should know about his discovery. It would be his legacy."

Gabriel nodded, about to say something reassuring, but Velda didn't let him speak. She pressed her lips to his and seconds later, whatever thoughts he'd been entertaining went out of his head entirely.

Chapter 9

"There," Nils said, pointing across the icy wasteland. "On the left, about ten o'clock."

Gabriel squinted through the Spryte's frosty windshield in the direction that Nils was pointing. At first he saw nothing but white, but then, as the noisy vehicle drew closer, he spotted a long, twisting swirl of crimson in the ice, like a bloodstain left by a slaughtered giant. It was a similar shade of red to the bone-fire in the Transdniestrian fortress, actually—as if the brick red flames had somehow been frozen in the ice. The carmine depths even seemed to flash and sparkle as they approached.

"This is the ice that Dr. Silver was sampling when he disappeared," Nils said, slowing and then stopping the Spryte about a hundred yards from the site. "There are hidden crevasses all over this location, one of which undoubtedly claimed the life of Dr. Silver. These are an anomaly—there are normally no such crevasses found in this area. The rescue team has already explored many of them, but no . . ." He looked at Velda, then turned away, squinting through the windshield. "No traces of Dr. Silver were found."

Velda's lovely face was stoic inside the pale frame of her fur-lined parka hood.

"We go on foot from here," Nils said. "It's not wise to bring the Spryte any closer. We will need to gear up and rope together before we start, just as if this were a glacier climb. I want everyone in harnesses and crampons—and remember to flatten out and anchor with your ice axe if one of us goes down, so that we don't all get pulled down after."

Nils opened the door to the Spryte, stepped out onto the ice and promptly disappeared from sight.

"Nils!" Gabriel cried, leaning across the Spryte to the driver's side to look out the open door.

The moment he shifted his weight, he felt the boxy vehicle shift with him, the driver's side dipping dramatically as a series of sharp cracks and a long low rumble sounded from beneath them.

"Everyone, shift to the right!" Gabriel said, pushing himself back against the passenger side door. "To the right! Millie, move—we need your weight." The big man threw himself against the side of the vehicle. "Come on. As far over as you can or this thing is going down and taking us with it."

For an unbearably tense moment, the Spryte rocked slowly back and forth as if deliberating their fate. No one said a word. The only movement inside the cab came from the swirling clouds of their anxious, steaming breath. Then, slowly, the rocking eased and the vehicle seemed to even out, balanced with the left side only slightly lower than the right. The slant was enough that Gabriel could now see out the open door. The frozen crust that Nils had fallen through now sported a jagged, three-foot-wide crack.

"Nils!" Gabriel called. "Can you hear me?"

For a minute, they heard nothing but the howl of the wind. Then as if from a great distance, a tiny, echoing voice answered.

"I'm alive." Gabriel saw Velda's eyes slide shut with relief. "I'm on a . . . a kind of steep ledge. Very slick . . . can't get much of a grip. I suspect I will fall if I shift my weight even slightly."

"Okay," Gabriel said, his mind racing. "Okay. Just hang on. We're going to figure out a way to get you out of there."

He turned back to where Millie, Velda and Rue were squeezed together in the far right-hand side of the rear seat.

"Listen," he said. "One of us needs to try and reach the gear in the back. We need to grab the packs and get out of the Spryte before it falls."

"I'll do it," Rue said. "I'm the lightest."

"Fine," Gabriel said. "Go." He pressed his body back against the passenger-side door as Rue carefully began crawling toward the packs behind her. As she closed her fingers around the strap of the closest pack, the Spryte shifted again, tilting precariously. Gabriel leaned back hard to counterbalance it and he saw Millie doing the same, but Rue lost her footing and tumbled against one of the rear doors. She grabbed the frame as the door swung open, barely avoiding falling out and into the crevasse. The pack was not so lucky. It slid past Rue and out the open door.

A moment later, Nils's voice called up from below. "What was that?"

"Your pack," Gabriel shouted. "It didn't happen to land near you by any chance . . . ?"

"No," Nils said. "Gabriel?" There was a long echoing pause. "I'm becoming somewhat concerned about my situation."

"We're working on it," Gabriel said. What he didn't say was that he was becoming somewhat concerned about their situation, too. He could feel the Spryte still gently teetering and could hear the ice beneath them groaning. "All right," he said, "forget the packs. Everybody out. Rue, you go first, out this side."

"But Gabriel, if we don't have any supplies . . ." she began.

He cut her off. "No time to discuss it, Rue. We may only have seconds—"

But they didn't even have that.

They all felt it as the lip of the crevasse crumbled beneath the Spryte's weight. The vehicle tipped forward and smashed through the fragile surface. There was a silent instant where Gabriel felt suspended in midair, like a baseball at the top of its trajectory in that infinitely brief, motionless instant before the descent begins. And then they were plunging into darkness.

Gabriel felt himself thrown sideways, over the back of the driver's seat. He fell against the others in a tangle of limbs, heard Millie's grunt as their heads collided. The vehicle glanced off one sheer icy face of the crevasse and then the other before it came to an abrupt stop with a massive grinding crunch. They were tightly wedged between the narrowing walls of ice. The crevasse went on, as they could tell from the sound of chunks of ice continuing to fall into the darkness below—but the truck was too wide to fall any farther.

The faint light filtering down from above showed that the front end of the Spryte was smashed inward as if they had been in a severe head-on crash. If Gabriel had not been thrown into the backseat, he would have been pinned—or, more likely, crushed to death. The radio below the accordioned dashboard was twisted into useless scrap. The glove box had dropped open, dumping out a miscellany of maps and tools, including a large flashlight. Gabriel grabbed the flashlight and switched it on, driving back the blue gloom and illuminating the pale faces of the huddled team members.

"Everybody okay?" Gabriel asked. "Anyone hurt?"

Before anybody could answer there was a thud and a crash from above. Bits of safety glass rained down around them from a shattered window. Gabriel shone the flashlight upward to reveal a booted leg dangling through the window.

"Nils?" Gabriel said.

"I'm all right," Nils said, though his voice sounded otherwise, like he was speaking through gritted teeth.

Gabriel helped pull Nils down into the cabin. The big Swede was shaken and sported a bloody bruise on one cheek, but he seemed at least not to have any broken bones.

"You really thought jumping down here from that ledge was a good idea?" Gabriel said.

"I wish I could tell you that I did," Nils said, "and that this was all part of a clever plan on my part—but really it was the ledge's decision, not mine."

"Got it," Gabriel said. He shone the light upward. It only penetrated so far into the deep blue walls of ice. The sky was barely visible in the distance.

"We're going to have to try to free up some of the gear from the back and make the climb to the surface," Gabriel said. "Won't be easy, but we should be able to get back to the station on foot and then radio to the Pole for help. Nils, do you think you can make it?"

"I'm not sure," Nils said. "My leg—"

"I can do it," Velda said. "My father took me on tougher climbs than this when I was a kid."

Gabriel doubted it. Any father who'd take a child on a climb even half this hard would've deserved an arrest for endangerment. But Gabriel appreciated the attitude, and he wasn't about to turn down an offer for help. "All right. The rest of you stay here in the Spryte till we come back with a rescue team. We'll go as quickly as we can."

"Don't go quickly," Rue said. "Go safely."

"That, too," Gabriel said. "But in this weather, slow's not safe. Not for any of us."

Nils reached into his jacket and fished out a poker hand of Hershey bars from an inner pocket. "Before you go. Some calories."

Gabriel grabbed two of the bars, passed one to Velda. They were rock hard.

"Break it into squares," Nils said, "and hold each square in your mouth until it's warm enough to chew."

Gabriel did as Nils suggested, sucking on the chocolate in the icy blue twilight. In the depths of the crevasse, out of the shrieking wind on the surface, they were cocooned in a churchlike silence. It was tempting to stay here, huddled together for warmth. But it wouldn't take long for the chocolate to run out, and, shortly after that, the warmth.

"Right," Gabriel said around the last mouthful of chocolate. "Let's see if we can free up that gear."

Velda's pack came free fairly easily from the rear of the Spryte but the remaining three were stuck fast, clenched in the crumpled metal as if between teeth. Millie was able to reach his pack and unzip it a few inches. He emptied it of a few smaller items through the opening, passed them to Gabriel. The other two packs were hopelessly inaccessible.

Gabriel and Velda strapped themselves into climbing harnesses and Gabriel readied a pick in one hand.

Rue, meanwhile, was poking around the ruined dashboard. "I might be able to get the heat up and running in here," she said. "But I'm afraid that would melt the ice around us and send us who knows how much farther down."

"Don't do it unless you absolutely have to," Gabriel said.

"We'll be fine," Nils said. "Just come back swiftly."

Gabriel pushed himself up, using the back of the driver's seat for leverage. He was about to stick his head out through the smashed rear window when Velda said, "Wait, what's that sound?"

The team was silent, listening. Gabriel heard nothing at first and then a low, distant rumble that grew rapidly louder and louder.

"Oh, no," Nils said.

"What?" Gabriel said.

His voice was a whisper. "Avalanche."

Chapter 10

Before Gabriel could react, a crushing wave of jagged ice slammed into the Spryte with the impact of a speeding train, wedging the vehicle down deeper into the crevasse and blotting out the pale, distant sun. Several smaller chunks of ice smashed down through the broken window before one too large to fit sealed it up completely.

The rumbling grew fainter and more muffled as more and more ice piled up on top of the Spryte. Eventually it ceased. The Spryte's battered steel hull groaned and creaked in protest against the added weight.

"Jesus," Millie said softly.

"All right," Gabriel said. "Change of plans." He shone the flashlight down through the front windshield, revealing the outlines of a narrow black chasm below them. "If we can't go up, we have to go down. We'll rappel down to the bottom, see if there isn't a way up and around the piled-up ice."

"If there *is* a bottom," Rue said.

"Spoken like a true optimist," Millie muttered.

"Tie a rope to the frame of the Spryte," Nils said. "Those without harnesses can just slide down."

"Good idea." Gabriel tossed a length of neon green rope to Velda, who swiftly knotted it to the frame. Gabriel made his way down to the windshield and with one swift kick knocked the glass from its frame. He listened to its fall. One second, two . . . then the crash as it splintered against the ice. There was a bottom.

Velda came down beside him, aiming the flashlight through the windshield. "Here," she said, "hold this," and handed him the light. "I'll go first."

Normally, Gabriel might have insisted that he be the first one down, out of some atavistic sense of chivalry or propriety. But he owed it to Rue and Millie to get them down safely—he'd dragged them into this, after all. "Okay," he said. "Just be careful."

Velda leaned forward awkwardly from her crouch and planted a kiss on Gabriel's chin. She found his lips with her second attempt. "I'm always careful." Then she was gone, making her way down the rope into the blackness.

Half a minute passed in silence. Then they heard Velda's voice. "I'm down!"

"Is it stable?" Gabriel called.

"Yes." Another long moment of silence. "Can you send down the light?"

Gabriel hauled up the rope, tied it tightly around the shaft of the flashlight, and without turning it off began lowering it. They watched the yellow cone of light reflecting off the ice walls, bright at first and then fainter and fainter as it descended. Eventually the line was fully paid out. "Hang on," Velda called, "keep it steady . . . got it." She was far enough below them that they could only see the faintest glow. Her voice, when it next came, was quieter, as if she'd gone some distance away. "There's a . . . a passageway, a narrow one. It looks like it could lead into another crevasse."

"Any sign of a way back up to the surface?" Gabriel called.

"Not yet."

"Well, it can't be any worse than what we've got here," Gabriel said. He gestured toward Nils. "I'll tie the rope under your arms, lower you down."

"I can lower myself," Nils said, climbing awkwardly down onto the driver's seat.

"All right," Gabriel said.

The tall Swede took hold of the rope and dropped through the windshield, rappelling downward against the ice wall.

"Nils is coming down," Gabriel called. "Help him off at the bottom."

Moments later, they heard a cry of pain as Nils touched down. "Got him," Velda shouted.

"Everything okay?" Gabriel said.

"Just my ankle," Nils shouted. "It'll be fine."

"Not broken?"

"No, just twisted."

As they spoke, Gabriel hauled the rope back up, tied Velda's pack to the end, and lowered it. He felt a series of tugs at the bottom as Velda undid the knots, then a lightening as she pulled the pack off. He repeated the maneuver, sending down a bundle of loose gear tied up in Millie's sleeping bag.

"Here's the rest," he shouted.

Again, the wait, then Velda's voice.

"Got it."

"Okay, Rue," Gabriel said. "Your turn."

Rue looked doubtfully down the rope and back up at Gabriel.

"I'll hold it steady," Gabriel said.

"Great." She took hold of the rope with both gloved hands, but didn't begin letting herself down.

"Time to go," Gabriel said.

"I'm going!" she replied indignantly. "What, do you think I'm scared?"

"If you are—" Gabriel began, but before the words were out she was shimmying down the rope into the chasm, the bright red of her parka slowly swallowed up by the blackness.

He held on tightly to the top of the rope, trying to minimize its torsion as she descended. "You doing okay?" he called after a minute of unbroken silence.

"What do you think?" Rue called back. "If I wasn't, you'd've heard me screaming." A moment later, she called, "I'm down." Then: "Man! It's cold as hell down here. When we get out of this, you owe me a trip to a goddamn hot spring, Hunt."

Gabriel smiled and slapped Millie's big meaty shoulder. "You ready?"

"You know," Millie said, his steaming breath labored as he grabbed hold of the rope, "the town I grew up in is only seven feet above sea level. Seven feet, Gabriel. I can't help but ask myself what the hell a decent God-fearing Chalmetian like me is doing freezing his ass off and making like a yoyo at twenty-eight-hundred feet. It ain't natural, I tell you."

"Go on, you big baby," Gabriel said.

"How do I keep letting you talk me into this kind of thing?" Millie asked, lowering himself hand over big hand down the rope, which swayed despite Gabriel's best efforts to hold it steady. "I oughta have my head examined."

The Spryte groaned and shifted under Millie's considerable weight on one end and the even greater weight of the piled-up ice on the other. A sudden lurch shook the vehicle. Gabriel tasted an icy metallic fear in the back of his throat. The rope bearing Millie's weight swung to one side and a barrage of colorful swearing echoed up the chasm.

"Don't want to rush you," Gabriel called down, "but . . . shake a leg, okay?"

"What's happening up there, boss?"

The groaning and creaking was getting louder, and though the darkness was now almost complete, by peering closely Gabriel could see the metal frame of the Spryte bulging inward. "Not your problem. Just get down."

Suddenly, Gabriel felt the rope jerk in his hands. There was no weight on it anymore. A moment later, he heard a heavy impact. "What happened?" he shouted.

"I got down," Millie called. "Figured I could stand to drop the last dozen feet or so. Wasn't the slickest landing ever, but I'm in one piece. Now you, boss. Get your ass down here."

Gabriel didn't need to be told twice. He took hold of the rope and pushed off, sliding down as quickly as he could into the blackness. His head was aching from the altitude and his breath was leaden in his constricted chest but he pushed all that aside and concentrated only on lowering himself into the chasm.

Above him, he heard the sound of metal twisting, and he felt the motion transmitted through the rope. The Spryte couldn't fall any farther—could it?

It was a chance he couldn't afford to take. He slackened his grip on the rope and slid, as quickly as he was able. He could feel the walls of ice narrowing around him until he had to twist his body sideways in order to slip down between them. Another noise came from above, the sound of metal snapping this time—and a moment later, there was no tension in the rope at all. It had been severed, and Gabriel was falling.

Chapter 11

There was a moment of blind plummeting, the useless rope still gripped between his hands. Then he hit—but where'd he'd expected to strike solid ice, he felt something soft under him instead. Millie's arms wrapped around him from behind and set him down gently on the ground.

Velda swung the light around.

They were in a long narrow corridor of ancient ice that glowed blue in the flashlight's glare. Above their heads, the crack leading up to the crushed Spryte was the only opening. Everything else was sealed solid, the ice bulging around them in an oval pocket that was disturbingly reminiscent of the spine and ribs of some enormous animal, viewed from the inside. Only in one direction was there any way they could go—and who knew how far?

"What do you think, Nils?" Gabriel asked. "Think there may be another way up? Nils?"

The big Swede was bent over, sorting through a pile of smashed equipment scattered across the ground. It was the contents of the first pack, Gabriel realized, the one that had fallen out of the Spryte when they were still aboveground, the one that had plummeted past

Nils while he'd been clinging to the ice ledge. Nils was gathering up what he could, sorting the hopelessly broken from the salvageable.

"Velda," Nils said, excitedly. "Look at this. These are not mine." He held up a pair of broken goggles.

Velda took the goggles from him and examined them up close in the flashlight's beam.

"They're his!" she said, her voice shaking. "They are, aren't they?"

"I think you might be right," Nils replied. "They certainly look like your father's. I don't think any of the rescue team lost their goggles while searching, and no one else has been anywhere near this area recently that we know of."

"So he must have been down here," Velda said, almost to herself. She swung the flashlight around. "His last transmission, it must have been from here . . ."

"Then where's his radio?" Gabriel said. He didn't add, *And where's his body?*

Velda aimed the light toward the passageway at the far end. "Nowhere else he could've gone."

"By an amazing coincidence, there's also nowhere else we can," Rue said. "Who's up for a walk? It's too damn cold just standing around."

Millie used the severed rope to rig a strap for his bundle and slung it over his shoulder. Hunched over to pass under the low roof of ice, he made his way to Rue's side. Velda stood silent for a moment, holding the goggles and looking away down the dark tunnel. She put the goggles into her pack, then shouldered it.

"Let's do it," she said.

Gabriel nodded and took his place by her side. Nils brought up the rear, not too badly slowed by his limp or his need to walk bent over almost double due to his height.

The natural corridor narrowed and widened as they went, twisting first to the left and then back to the right. They came to a section where the ceiling got so low that even Rue had to bend over to keep walking, and then it became lower still. They were forced to creep forward first on their hands and knees and then on their bellies, pushing the packs ahead of them. As they inched forward, Gabriel noticed that the ice beneath them was becoming a downward slope, gradual at first, then increasingly steep. Gabriel could feel himself starting to slide. He had to arch his back and wedge himself against the ceiling as he went, to prevent himself from slipping.

"Can you see anything?" Gabriel asked Velda, who was in the lead with the flashlight.

Before she could answer there was a grunt and a cry and both Millie and Rue came sliding down behind them, slamming into Gabriel and sending him head-first into Velda's boots. The four of them slipped and slid and bounced off one another until they hit the bottom of the slope, wind knocked soundly from their aching lungs.

Standing unsteadily, Gabriel picked up the flashlight from where it lay. The light was flickering, and he had to slap it twice before it returned to a full, steady beam.

He shone the light around the room. It was an enormous cavern, the walls composed entirely of the curious red ice they'd seen on the surface. The roof was perhaps seventy-five feet overhead and angled sharply. Thousands of glittering crimson stalactites hung from it, some finger-sized, some well over forty feet long. They were not smooth and rounded like traditional stalactites, but sharp-edged and faceted, like giant crystals. Equally varied and equally sharp stalagmites reached upward from the floor of the cavern. The resulting impression was that of standing inside a cathedral-sized geode.

"It's . . . amazing," Velda said. The surfaces of the strange, mineral-laden red ice seemed to pick up the tone of her voice and resonate until the resulting cacophony was almost unbearable. As the sound swelled and echoed, a few smaller stalactites came loose from the ceiling and rained down around them like crystal daggers. One caught Millie on the arm, slicing easily through his parka sleeve. He pulled his arm back with a sudden intake of breath. He bit down on a hiss of pain but the short, truncated sound was picked up and relayed all across the cavern and back again, as if whispered by gossiping old ladies.

Nils appeared then, crawling through the narrow tunnel the rest of them had exited in an uncontrolled, headlong rush. He began to say something but Gabriel held his finger to his lips and shook his head. Nils nodded and remained silent. Even the faint sound of their breathing was amplified, every facet of every crystal humming with each exhalation. Scanning across the room silently, Gabriel could make out a tall, narrow opening in the opposite wall. It was the only way out he could see. They were going to have to make their way across to that opening—and they'd have to do it without uttering a single sound.

The razor-edged stalagmites made a straight shot across the cavern impossible, their jutting facets turning the ground of the cavern into a particularly nasty labyrinth. After seeing what a tiny one had done to Millie's thick parka, Gabriel was quite sure he didn't want to brush against any of them by accident. Carefully, he began to pick his way along a circuitous, spiraling route that avoided the densest patches of crystals. He waved for the others to follow.

They followed, and spoke not a word. But even their cautious, sliding footsteps were amplified to an accusatory racket by the singing crystals.

They'd made it nearly three-quarters of the way across when Rue lost her footing on the slick ice. She reached out instinctively for balance and gripped one of the nearest stalagmites. The sharp edge sliced open the palm of her glove and slid deep into the flesh of her hand. A high-pitched yelp of pain escaped from her throat before she could stifle it.

For a second, the team stood frozen as the sound doubled and quadrupled into a jagged siren wail echoing through the crystalline chamber. First the smallest crystals and then larger ones began to detach and drop all around them.

"Run!" Gabriel spat in a harsh constricted whisper that was immediately snatched up and echoed back by the crystals.

They made a break for the narrow opening, tearing at top speed through the deadly rain of crystal blades. The clashing racket had become so loud and piercing that Gabriel had to cover his ears as he ran, the pain in his eardrums outweighing even the sting of the cuts inflicted by the falling crystals.

When Gabriel made it to the shelter of the tunnel opening, he reached out to grab Velda and Rue, pulling them to safety. Millie was close behind but Nils had fallen about twelve feet back, a foot-long crystal piercing his calf like an arrow.

Millie turned back, dodging the falling crystals, and swiftly hauled the silent, bleeding Swede up in his arms. Gabriel clenched his fists as Millie darted and weaved, eyes cast up at the ceiling, trying to guess where the next deadly missile would plunge.

One fell directly in front of him, smashing to shrapnel against the ground, the sound of its impact setting off sympathetic vibrations in the crystals all around the point of impact. Millie kicked a large fragment out of his path, put his head down, and barreled forward. He made it into the tunnel just seconds before a truly massive stalactite, as wide around as Millie himself and twice as tall, came crashing down. It fell against the tunnel entrance, sealing it. The terrible screaming of the resonating crystals was muffled at last.

Gabriel looked around as Millie set Nils down on the ground. This tunnel was also roofed with the glittering red ice—but here the ice was smooth and flat, not lined with crystals. He laid one palm against the nearest wall. No vibrations, even when he quietly whispered, "Testing . . . testing . . ." He tried it louder. Nothing happened.

"It's okay, we can talk," Gabriel said. His voice sounded muted and distant in his ringing ears. "Everybody all right?"

"Man, that stings," Rue said, holding up her cut hand and poking at the slash in her glove.

"I'm okay," Velda said. "How's Nils?"

The team gathered around the fallen Swede.

"I am all right," Nils said. "It is not so very bad."

Gabriel bent close and examined the crystal protruding from Nils's calf.

"I need to pull it out," Gabriel said. "But first I'll need something to handle it with so I don't cut my fingers."

Millie unslung his bedroll and pulled out a heavy pair of pliers. Gabriel took them from him and positioned the jaws on either side of the crystal. "Good news is," he told Nils, "something this sharp ought to come out cleanly. You ready?"

The Swede nodded. "Yes. I am ready."

Gabriel gently squeezed the pliers closed. He pulled on the crystal and it came free with a moist, smacking sound. A heavy flow of blood followed. Gabriel motioned to Velda.

"Quick," he said. "Get the first aid kit out of your pack."

She dug through her pack while Gabriel rolled up the leg of Nils' freezer suit and applied direct pressure on the wound. When Velda handed him the first aid kit, he was able to quickly clean and bandage the cut.

"How about me, doc?" Rue said, holding her palm out to Gabriel.

Gabriel spent the next half hour playing doctor, checking and cleaning everyone's slices and scratches, including his own. By the time he had everyone bandaged up, he was beginning to feel light-headed and exhausted.

"We need to eat again," Nils said from where he sat propped up against one wall. "And rest."

Gabriel didn't argue. Millie set to work chipping ice while Nils rationed out a handful of energy bars he'd salvaged from his pack. They laid out the three sleeping bags they had—Nils's, Velda's and Millie's—and agreed that they would sleep in shifts. Millie volunteered to take the first shift up and handed his sleeping bag over to a grateful Gabriel. Rue offered to join Millie and the two of them sat huddled together by the blocked mouth of the tunnel, talking softly about their

favorite food while chewing the dry, tasteless energy
bars and washing them down with ice melt.

Gabriel looked over at Velda, but she did not return
his glance. She seemed sealed up inside herself, utterly
single-minded and driven. There was certainly no hint
of invitation as she bedded down on the far side of the
tunnel and rolled over with her back to him. It was as
if Gabriel had imagined the intimacy they'd shared
back at the research station.

But he was too tired to give Velda's behavior a second thought. The instant he pulled off his boots and
zipped himself into Millie's huge sleeping bag, he fell
into a deep and comforting dreamless sleep.

Chapter 12

When Millie woke him, Gabriel felt disoriented and dehydrated, a feeling not unlike a bad hangover. He dragged himself upright and slipped his altitude-swollen feet back into his too-tight boots, grunting wordlessly as Millie slid into the sleeping bag in his place. Staggering down the tunnel to empty his aching bladder, Gabriel still felt foggy and half asleep. He kept going till he was a good, respectful distance away from the others and leaned against the wall with one hand while he struggled with the other through far too many layers of snaps, buttons and zippers. By the time he was able to begin relieving himself against the wall, Gabriel found that he was flushed and damp with sweat from the effort. He realized that while it was certainly still cold here, it was substantially warmer than it had been back by the tunnel's mouth. The wall against which he was leaning felt like rough stone beneath a thin crust of ice, not the solid ice of the section in which they'd slept.

Curious, he headed farther along the tunnel, head cocked and listening. He could have sworn he'd heard—yes, there it was, at the edges of his hearing, a delicate trickling sound.

Running water.

He came around a bend and discovered a tiny, winding stream flowing along a deep groove in the ice.

Gabriel rushed back to the mouth of the tunnel, where he found Nils awake and melting chips of ice over a camp stove.

"Nils," Gabriel said. "There's a stream up ahead. About fifty yards down the tunnel."

"What?" Nils stood, frowning. "That's not possible. It's far too cold for liquid water here."

"Well, it's warmer there," Gabriel said. "Much warmer than it is here."

At the word "warmer" Velda was wide-awake and on her feet.

"It's just like my father said. We must be getting closer to the place he found. The place he vanished." She jammed her feet into her boots and hastily began rolling her sleeping bag.

"Hold on a minute," Gabriel said, keeping his voice low. He motioned to Millie and Rue, both of whom were still sleeping. "We need to let them rest for a while first."

"No time to rest," Velda said. "Not when we're this close. Not when my father's been on his own here for weeks—maybe sick or hurt, starving. No. We're going."

Gabriel watched Velda shoulder her pack and head down the passage. Nils bent to turn off and pack up the stove. He offered Gabriel a drink of meltwater from the small tin pot and Gabriel accepted gratefully.

"Better wake the others," Nils said.

Millie and Rue were not happy to be dragged from their sleeping bags.

"Who the hell put her in charge?" Rue grumbled, when Gabriel had explained.

"She's right about her father," Gabriel said. "If he's

still alive, he needs help. And we can't let her go on alone."

"*You* can't let her go on alone," Rue said. "She's not smoking *my* joint."

"We must all stay together," Nils said. "Going alone down here is suicide. That's how Lawrence vanished."

"So this way we can all vanish together," Rue said. "Much better." But she tugged on her boots.

Millie came up behind her. "Man, Rue, you're getting grouchy in your old age. What'd you think you were getting into when Gabriel called and said, 'Wanna go to the South Pole?' A five-star hotel with a feather bed and a down comforter—"

"Ah, fuck you, Millie," Rue snarled, "and your down comforter. I'm a driver. You see anything down here for me to drive? No. I don't know what the hell I'm doing here." She gave Gabriel a big false smile. "So, we going, or what?"

Gabriel led the way down the passage after Velda. They followed the stream a hundred yards and found her crouching beside it.

"It's water all right," she said, pulling off her glove and scooping up a handful to drink. "It's cold as hell, but it's water. It's real."

Gabriel bent down and took a drink from the stream. It was deeper here than the little trickle he'd first spotted, and the water was cold, fresh and delicious. He could feel his dehydrated body soak up every drop and beg for more. But it was still too cold to expose his bare skin to it for long—his hand felt almost as if it were burning where it had touched the water, and he had no choice but to dry it off as quickly as possible and tuck it up under his parka.

Nils brought out the tin cup and they took turns

filling and emptying it. When the team had all had enough, they set out to follow the stream. It bubbled along the left side of the narrow tunnel, sometimes shallow enough that you could see the stone bed beneath the water, sometimes deep and wide enough to cover almost the entire floor of the tunnel, forcing the team to walk single-file along a skinny strip of higher ground against the right-hand wall.

Gabriel was beginning to lose track of time in the dim unchanging sameness of the tunnel. Even though he had slept, he still felt tired. It was far too easy to lose focus, and at one point he nearly lost his footing as well, his boot coming within inches of plunging into the icy stream.

"Careful," Nils said, gripping Gabriel's upper arm and steadying him. "It may be warmer down here than on the surface, but it's still cold enough that you do not want to have a wet boot. I can tell you from personal experience that frostbite is nothing you want to become familiar with."

Gabriel was suddenly keenly aware of the missing fingers on the hand that gripped his arm. He nodded, and continued carefully along the edge of the stream.

About thirty minutes later, the tunnel opened into a wide, high-ceilinged ice cave. There, the little stream ended, depositing its flow of water into a rushing underground river, more than twenty feet wide and disturbingly deep. Peering down into the water, Gabriel could see, beneath the spume and froth on the surface, several sharply crenellated columns of ice plunging vertiginously downward into what seemed no less than a water-filled canyon. The river traveled sinuously around several small humped islands of ice—some of them large and bulky, some as small as manhole covers back in New York—before disappearing into a crevice on the far side of the cave. To the left of the crevice was the entrance to another small tunnel. On the right side of the river—the side they were on—was a dead end, the path they'd been following coming to an abrupt halt against a wall of ice.

"That tunnel looks like the only way forward," Gabriel said. "And I think it's fair to say that swimming across is right out."

"Without dry suits and specialized diving gear?" Nils said. "Hypothermia would set in almost immediately. Even if you made it across, without a change of warm, dry clothing on the other side, death would not be long in coming."

"What about those?" Velda asked, pointing at the islands in the middle of the river. "Couldn't we work our way across using them as stepping stones?"

"Maybe you could," Rue said. "I've got shorter legs."

"I'll go," Gabriel said. "I'll carry one of the ropes across. You anchor one end here, I'll anchor the other in the wall over there, and that'll give the rest of you a guide line to hold onto. Rue, you can even go hand over hand if there are gaps that are too wide for you to step across."

"Do we both remember the condition my hand's in?" Rue said. "I know I do."

"Seeing as how I bandaged it for you, I think I do, too," Gabriel said. "But unless you've got a better plan to suggest . . ."

"All right," Rue said after a moment, kicking a fragment of ice into the water. "I'll do it. But you anchor that rope tight, you understand?"

Chapter 13

With the rope spooled over his shoulder and Millie holding onto the other end, Gabriel stepped out onto the first of the ice islands. The surface was damned slippery—even with his spike-soled boots, Gabriel found himself sliding and had to put his arms out to either side for balance. He didn't look back. He didn't need to see the faces of the other team members to envision the looks of concern he knew they'd be wearing. What he needed to do was to concentrate. He took a series of slow, deep breaths and steadied himself. The nearest island was just two feet away on a diagonal—he could make that one easily. Rotating slowly, slowly, till he was facing the other island, Gabriel balanced, raised one leg and shifted forward.

His foot landed squarely, the spikes biting into the ice. But as he brought his other leg across, he felt himself teeter and start to fall. Behind him, he heard someone gasp. He swung his arms up and corrected his balance, throwing his weight to the opposite side. Concentrate, he told himself. Focus. There's no one here, there's no water, there's no river, there's just your feet and these islands, and you either make it across or you're dead.

Once he was steady again, he looked across to the

far side, mapping the shortest path from here to there. Five more islands. Five more chances to fall.

He stepped across to the next island, one of the largest, and rested there for a moment. It was big enough he could even have sat down, but he didn't. No point trying to get comfortable on a frozen, slippery surface, least of all when you had four more ahead of you.

The next crossing went smoothly. He heard Millie call out for him to stop and then felt a slight tug on the rope coiled on his shoulder. "Got your angle now," Millie shouted. Gabriel could hear him hammering a piton into the wall and attaching his end of the rope to it. Gabriel waited till the hammering ended and Millie shouted, "All clear," before taking a careful step across to the fourth island.

This time Gabriel did chance a look back over his shoulder. He was a bit more than halfway across. It felt strange, standing on a tiny, ice-crusted rock with a deadly torrent of water rushing by just inches away from his feet. The bigger problem, though, was that he only had two more tiny, ice-crusted rocks left, to cross nearly the same amount of space that he'd had four islands to get him across so far. There'd be no more stepping across from here on—these two would require jumps, and jumping from one icy surface to another, with zero tolerance for error . . .

He steadied himself, aimed, and leapt, landing squarely in the center of the island. But it wasn't a flat surface—what he hadn't been able to see from where he'd jumped was that on the far side the ice was canted steeply to the right. He found himself pitching forward. He tried to lean back, but he couldn't—too much momentum was dragging him forward, downward, toward the water—

Then he felt a mighty tug on his shoulder and found himself lifted off his feet, like a fish on the end of a line. "No you don't," Millie shouted. "You stay outta that water, y'hear?" And Gabriel landed flat on his back on the surface of the little island. He felt himself start slipping again and spun onto his belly, scrabbling with the palms of his gloves for purchase. Gabriel stopped his skid and lay facedown on the ice, gripping tightly with all four limbs. "Thanks," he said, too quietly to be heard. But Millie knew he'd said it and called back, "Ain't nothin', brother."

Slowly, Gabriel rose to his knees, brushing off the surface of his parka as best he could. It was wet, maybe even dangerously so—but a hell of a lot less so than it might have been.

Gabriel re-coiled the rope, replaced it around his shoulder, and got to his feet.

"You sure you're okay?" Velda called.

"No," Gabriel said, and bent his knees for the next jump. He landed unevenly and had to take a step forward to keep his balance. But he kept it. "But if you wait till you're sure about things," he shouted, "you'll never get out of bed in the morning." He jumped from the island to the far shore and, pulling the rope tight, secured it to a piton he hammered into a cleft in the wall. The rope now stretched across the river, within easy reach of five of the six islands and not completely out of reach of the sixth.

He cupped his hands on either side of his mouth. "So, who's first?"

Millie was the last to cross. Rue had gone hand over hand most of the way, relieving some of the pressure on her injured palm by using her legs as well, crossed at the ankles over the rope. Velda had crossed carefully, measuring each jump. And then Nils had gone, his long stride making several of the crossings easier for him than any of the others had found them.

Then it was Millie's turn. He avoided putting his weight on the rope, not only because he was the heaviest by far but because there was no one left on the far shore to hold onto the rope if it came free from its mooring.

He made it to the last island without incident—a few tense moments, but he kept his head and his balance. But then as he landed on the surface of the final island, his foot slipped. His free arm pinwheeled for balance as he gripped the rope. It dipped low under his weight and before he could right himself, he plunged one leg into the water up to the knee.

"GodDAMN," he hollered, yanking his foot back up as if he'd dipped it into boiling oil and nearly overbalancing the other way.

"Hang on," Gabriel called, hauling on the rope with all his weight to keep it up while Millie leaned against it. "You're almost across."

Millie regained his balance and then jumped the last six feet to the bank. Gabriel and Nils reached out to catch him and haul him away from the river's edge.

"Get his boot off," Nils said. "Quickly."

Gabriel pulled off Millie's boot and dripping sock and then took off his own parka and wrapped it around Millie's cold, corpse-pale foot. Nils pulled out a knife from his pack and began cutting sections from Millie's sleeping bag, an L-shaped corner piece and a batch of narrow strips. While Gabriel rubbed warmth back into Millie's icy foot, Nils cobbled together a temporary foot covering for Millie to wear while his boot dried.

"Damn that was close," Millie said, letting out a

long shaky breath. "I never realized how much I like having ten toes until just now."

Nils tied the makeshift boot onto Millie's foot and helped him up, handing the parka back to Gabriel.

"Can you walk like that?" Gabriel asked.

"Remember that time in San Borja, with the hot tar?" Millie said. "Compared to that, this is a piece of cake."

"Just the same," Gabriel said, and put an arm across the big man's waist. Millie didn't object and leaned on him heavily as they headed into the narrow tunnel.

As they went, Gabriel started to notice veins of exposed rock peeking through gaps in the ice on the walls and ceiling. And after a series of snaking hairpin turns and switchbacks, the team found themselves in an entirely different type of cave.

It was long and narrow, approximately the size and shape of the interior of a school bus—but that was not what was unusual. What was unusual was the fact that the walls had no ice on them at all. It was solid rock on every side. It was also warmer, uncomfortably so.

At the far end of the cave was a crooked, vertical crack that looked like it wouldn't be wide enough to admit Millie unless he turned sideways and held his breath. Beside the crack was a heap of broken rock.

"Look," Gabriel said, pointing to a bit of neon green fabric barely visible beneath the rubble.

Velda made a soft, anguished sound in her throat and ran to the pile, dropping to her knees. She began moving pieces of stone off the fabric, revealing it to be the sleeve of a thermal parka.

"It's empty!" Velda cried, pulling the parka from beneath the rocks. She pointed to the large, indelible marker letters above the label that read SILVER. "It's my father's." She frowned and gripped the parka's collar tighter. "He couldn't last thirty minutes without this on the surface. Why would he take it off?"

"Same reason I'm about to," Gabriel said. He was starting to sweat profusely under his many thermal layers. The ambient temperature in the cave had to be nearly fifty degrees. He unzipped his parka and removed his gloves. "Can't you feel how much warmer it's getting?"

Nils unzipped as well. "We must be near some kind of previously undetected geothermic anomaly."

"You think it's warm there," Rue said, having slipped easily into the crack in the rock wall. "Check this out. This is where the warm air's coming from."

Gabriel walked over, stuck his hand inside. Sure enough.

"Listen," he said. "We need to take some of our gear off or we'll get overheated—but we can't leave it behind. We may not be able to return the way we came."

"No problem," Millie said. "I can carry the lot of 'em."

"We'll each carry our own," Gabriel said, squeezing his parka into a compact bundle.

The other team members quickly stripped out of their freezer suits, but the polar fleece pullovers and pants beneath were still much too warm for the inexplicably balmy temperature inside the cave. Even stripped down to their last layer of high-tech, lightweight, moisture-wicking thermals, they still felt sticky and overheated.

"Shh," Velda said, pausing from trying to force the zipper shut on her now overstuffed pack and putting a finger to her lips. "Do you hear that?"

"What?" Mille asked, cocking his massive head.

"Sounds like . . ." Velda began.

Millie casually slapped at the back of his neck and Gabriel grabbed his thick wrist, eyes wide. Millie frowned quizzically as Gabriel turned the big man's hand over to reveal a squashed mosquito and tiny splotch of bright blood.

"A mosquito!" Velda said, her voice incredulous.

"So what?" Millie shrugged. "This little squirt ain't nothing compared to the blood-sucking bombers we got back home."

"There are no mosquitoes of any size at the South Pole," Nils said. "No insects at all, in fact."

Millie looked down at the minuscule corpse in his hand.

"Should we try to preserve it or something?" Millie asked. "I feel kinda bad now for squashing the only living insect ever found at the South Pole."

"Guys," Rue called from the depth of the tunnel. "I really think you ought to see this."

While the other four were marveling over the unfortunate mosquito, Rue had followed her curiosity down the tunnel. She had turned a sharp corner, so she could be heard but not seen.

Gabriel twisted sideways and entered the tunnel, motioning for the others to follow. Inside the tunnel it was not just warm, it was humid, as utterly the opposite of the bone-dry chill aboveground as could possibly be imagined. The air had an odor, a rich green loamy smell that told Gabriel that Dr. Silver had not been hallucinating in his final transmission. When he came to the dogleg bend in the tunnel, his eyes confirmed what his nose had already told him.

The tunnel widened to a broad triangular opening. Rue was standing in the opening, hands on her hips. The other four joined her and stood together in awed silence, regarding the valley below. It was green. Lushly, verdantly, impossibly green.

Chapter 14

From where the team stood, they could see the rippling, leafy canopy of what looked like thick, tangled jungle below them, surrounded on all sides by sheer granite cliffs. About ten feet down from the ledge on which they were gathered, the river spewed out of the cliff face as a misty, ethereal waterfall, spilling down into a clear green pool below. High above their heads was a vaulted ceiling of the curious red ice, giving the daylight filtering through it a ruddy, perpetual-sunset hue. In the distance, at the far end of the valley, there was a large, jagged crack in the rooflike ice dome, through which a bright slash of ordinary daylight spilled in. It was hard to judge its length from this distance, but the crack looked to Gabriel to be at least twenty feet wide and a hundred feet long. It also looked as if several massive plates of ice overlapped at that point, forming a kind of covered ramp leading up to the frozen world above. It could be a way out, but it was easily a half a mile above the ground. Even if they were able to scale one of the sheer cliff faces and reach the frozen ceiling, they would still need to somehow travel upside-down, geckolike, across the curved ice to make their way to the crack.

"You see?" Velda asked, breathless and husky with emotion as she took in the sight before them. "I knew it!"

"I see it," Nils said, his faded blue eyes wide. "But I don't believe it."

"How can a place like this exist?" Gabriel asked. He reached down to grab a handful of crackling fallen leaves. He let the warm wind swirl them away. "How has it been able to escape satellite detection for so long?"

"Perhaps the red ice covering this valley has properties that allow it to deflect geothermal imaging?" Nils said. "I don't know."

"What we do know," Velda said, "is that my father wasn't crazy. Can you imagine how much a discovery like this might be worth?"

"It's worth nothing if we don't get out of here alive," Rue said.

"What are you thinking, boss," Millie said, "make our way over to that crack there?"

"One step at a time," Gabriel said. "First let's get ourselves down from here."

Driving a piton to anchor their remaining rope, the team carefully rappelled down the cliff, following the edge of the waterfall to the jungle floor.

Once they were on the ground, Gabriel was able to take a closer look at the foliage surrounding the water. The majority of the tallest trees were a species of fragrant, silvery eucalyptus that Gabriel had never seen before. In the shorter scrub layer, he thought he recognized a variety of distinctly Tasmanian flora in addition to a couple more species he couldn't place. Everywhere he looked, his eye fell on something new and impossible. Mysterious, unfamiliar songbirds with flashing orange and gold wings. Heavy, lumbering beetles like walking jewels. Curious lizards and tiny possum-like marsupials with wary red eyes. Velda was right—the sheer magnitude of a discovery like this was impossible to calculate, nearly overwhelming. But Rue was right, too. It would all be worth nothing if they didn't find a way back to the surface.

"Look," Velda said. "A trail!"

She pointed to what appeared to be a narrow, winding path on the left, leading off into the verdant bush alongside a rill flowing with runoff from the pool.

"I'll take point," Gabriel said. "Millie, you take the rear."

Millie nodded, peeling the scraps of sleeping bag off his foot and pulling on his damp boot.

"Everybody stay close and keep your eyes open," Gabriel said. He pointed at an animal skittering into the undergrowth. "Some of these look like smaller prey animals, and that means something bigger is probably eating them."

"Great," Rue said as they started down the trail. "I'm gonna be the first person in history to be eaten by a jaguar at the South Pole."

"Come, come," Nils said, squinting and wiping sweat from his eyes. "There cannot be any jaguars here. It's just not possible."

"This whole place is impossible," Millie replied. "How much more impossible is a jaguar than a mosquito?"

They trekked in silence, sweating. Within ten minutes, they'd unzipped the sleeves off their thermal shirts. After twenty, the legs came off the thermal underwear. They packed away the stripped-off pieces, knowing they'd be sorry when they returned to the surface if they didn't.

"Nils," Velda said, watching the tall man as he limped along beside her. "Are you all right?"

He nodded, but it was clear that the heat was getting to him. It felt to Gabriel like the temperature was somewhere north of eighty degrees Fahrenheit, and after twenty minutes of marching, Nils was flushed and sweating profusely, his thinning blond hair plastered to his skull. Having spent the last fifteen years of his life at temperatures that rarely rose above zero, his ability to cope with the sudden shift to tropical weather was also barely above zero.

The team came to a bend in the path and Gabriel could see a deep ravine just off to one side. At the bottom of the ravine the small stream they'd been following flowed gracefully over mossy stones.

"Be careful," Gabriel said. "Looks like a bit of a drop over here."

"Should we refill our canteens?" Millie asked, looking down over the edge.

"I don't know if we'd be able to make it back up to the trail," Gabriel said. "The bank looks awfully muddy."

"Do you think the water here is safe to drink?" Velda asked Nils.

"No way to know," Nils replied, peeling off his shirt and using it to mop sweat from his flushed neck. "Strange bacteria, unknown contaminants . . . Show me a proper Antarctic setting, I can tell you anything you want to know—but I can't vouch for anything in this place."

Gabriel heard a rustle in the brush on the right side

of the path ahead and froze, one hand out to stop the team behind him. A large, wolflike creature stepped out of the underbrush about ten feet down the trail. It was lean and oddly proportioned, with a low, hunched back and thick, tan fur striped black across its hindquarters. Its ears were small and rounded and its snout long and sharp. It had small, alert dark eyes with black Cleopatra stripes at the outer corners, and it regarded Gabriel as if sizing him up to determine whether he was a threat or a meal.

Gabriel remained stationary, breathing slowly, and the animal took a wary step sideways and back, revealing two cubs of the same species. They were smaller, but only slightly, nearly full grown. The pair weaved anxiously from side to side, staying half hidden behind what Gabriel was guessing was their mother. The she-wolf suddenly emitted a growl, hissing aggressively, and then opened her long narrow jaw alarmingly wide to display ranks of formidable teeth.

Seeing this, Gabriel suddenly recognized the animal. It was the thin, gaping jaw that did it—he remembered a piece of archival film from 1933 featuring the last known footage of a now extinct marsupial predator known as the Tasmanian tiger. Extinct—yet here was that very creature, alive and well and not very happy to see Gabriel standing in her path.

His first impulse had been to reach for his gun, which he'd strapped on before they'd descended to the jungle floor; but now that he knew what the animal was he reached instead into the bundle he'd made of his cold weather gear, checking pockets and trying to remember where he'd stashed his camera. He found it and brought it out as the mother tiger stood up on her hind legs, propped up by her stiff tail in an odd, kangaroo-like stance. She stretched her head up high on her slender neck, seemingly looking over Gabriel's shoulder at something behind him. Before Gabriel could thumb the lens cap off his camera, the creature let out an alarmed, high-pitched cry and she and her offspring bounded away into the thick underbrush.

"What do you think she—" Gabriel began, but he didn't get a chance to finish as a giant beaked head burst through the foliage beside them, snapping at Millie and washing the team in a blast of hot carrion breath. Millie leapt back, grunting in surprise. Gabriel swapped the camera for his Colt as the creature barreled past them in single-minded pursuit of the fleeing tigers.

It was a bird of sorts, but enormous and clearly flightless, moving across the ground with an ungainly loping stride. The towering creature had to be at least nine feet tall, with a massive head topped by a crest of long red feathers and a hooked, eaglelike beak that was obviously designed for tearing flesh. Its stubby, useless wings were more than balanced out by legs as thick as tree trunks and wide, splayed feet ending in wicked talons, each easily as long as the *kindjal* now being studied in the Royal Museum.

The bird came to a stop as it realized its prey had eluded it—or at least that one set of prey had. It blinked and twisted its muscular neck back toward the group, lowering its head and regarding them with a pair of eyes the size of tennis balls.

For something so large, the bird was astonishingly fast. One second, it was ten feet away, and less than a heartbeat later, it was on them, homing in on the tallest target in the group. Gabriel fired a shot at its flank as it passed but he didn't figure on its speed and the bullet went wide. The beast landed upon Nils with a flurry of battering wings and slashing talons. The lanky Swede let out a scream as he found himself caught by the neck in the grip of the razor-sharp beak. The bird shook him like a terrier with a rat and then tossed him effortlessly into the air. It was a horrifying sight. He was dead before he hit the dirt, his throat carved open in a bloody gash, his neck clearly broken. The bird landed on his body, one enormous clawed foot on his chest. As Gabriel took aim for a second shot, the bird dipped down and casually bit off Nils's head, swallowing it whole.

Chapter 15

Gabriel pulled the trigger. This time the bullet struck home. But it seemed only to enrage the animal. It swiveled to face him, its beak dripping crimson, and then cocked its head slightly, sniffing, its interest piqued by Rue and Velda.

Gabriel fired again, the roar of the Colt drowning out the bird's cry. This time he'd aimed for the head, but his bullet ricocheted off the creature's thick armored skull like a BB off a brick wall. At least, Gabriel told himself, he'd gotten the bird's attention away from the women. It was facing him directly now, screaming out a challenge. Out of the corner of one eye, Gabriel saw Rue scamper up a nearby tree, with Velda close behind her. Then he saw the bird's powerful thighs flex. It was getting ready to charge. There might be time for one more shot, at most. Gabriel steadied his hand—but before he could pull the trigger, Millie bellowed and charged the giant bird from the side, leaping up onto its back and wrapping his thick arms around the bird's neck.

The bird let out an earsplitting cry of alarm and staggered backward, shaking its head from side to side. Millie refused to let go, wrapping his long legs around the base of the feathered neck and throwing wild hammerfists at the softer portion at the base of the bird's skull. It bucked like a bronco and reared back, trying to throw him off, but Millie held tight. Having failed to dislodge him through sheer force, the bird raced toward a wide-boled tree and spun, ramming Millie against the trunk. Millie held on through the first impact and the second, but his grip loosened and the third finally knocked him off.

Millie tumbled into the bush and Gabriel fired another shot at the bird to get its attention again. It reacted to the sound, leaping a foot in the air and coming down not quite close enough to reach Gabriel with a strike of its beak but not nearly far enough away for Gabriel to feel comfortable with his chances of survival. He didn't want to go the way Nils had gone, supper for this prehistoric predator.

Gabriel and the bird circled warily around each other, the bird hissing and snapping its beak while Gabriel put another bullet into its feathered bulk. It finally seemed to be weakening—it was bleeding now in several spots—but the .45 caliber Colt just didn't have the power for a kill shot on an animal this massive unless he could score a direct hit to the heart or brain. With only one bullet left in the chamber, Gabriel was running out of options.

"Get down!" Millie suddenly cried.

Gabriel dropped and rolled away as Millie came charging out of the brush with a boulder the size of a laundry basket held high above his head. With an enormous grunt, Millie hurled the rock, hitting the startled bird squarely in the breastbone. It squawked and stumbled backward, slipping and clawing for purchase on the rocky lip of the ravine.

Gabriel used his last bullet to blast the stones out from under the bird's desperate, clutching feet and it tumbled backward into the ravine, splashing loudly into the shallow water below.

Silence followed.

Gabriel got back to his feet, unsteadily. "Good lord," he said, as he fought to catch his breath. "What *was* that?"

"Biggest damn turkey I ever seen," Millie said.

"I owe you one," Gabriel said.

"Only fair, boss. I've owed you, plenty of times." Millie didn't seem to be noticeably the worse for wear; he wasn't even breathing hard. But Gabriel had seen the force with which he'd been smashed against the tree and he knew the big man had to be hurting.

"Come on," Millie said. "Let's go get the girls out of the tree."

Gabriel nodded, but he stepped toward the ravine instead. "Let's just make sure it's—"

With a roar, the huge beaked head sprang up over the edge of the ravine, like the world's biggest jack-in-the-box.

Millie swore softly. Gabriel gripped his now empty pistol, silently calculating the time it would take the bird to climb back up to the path versus the time it would take him to reach his bundle and the pocket containing more bullets. It didn't look good.

"Boys," Rue shouted from her perch up the nearby eucalyptus. "Get your asses up here *now*!"

They ran. Seconds later the creature was back on the trail and thundering after them. Gabriel leapt up into the lower branches of the eucalyptus, while Millie chose a sturdier specimen on the other side of the path. The bird snapped at Gabriel, catching his left boot and pulling it off his foot. The unfamiliar object did not strike the creature as edible and it spit the boot off to one side, shaking its head with a strangely human expression of distaste. Luckily, this gave Gabriel enough time to make it up from one tree branch to the next until he was beside Velda and well above the bird's reach.

"Thank god," she said, clutching Gabriel's arm. "I thought . . ."

"I'm sorry about Nils," Gabriel said.

Down below, the bird stretched its neck, beak snapping, but it could not reach them. It ducked its head, scratched at the dirt and turned away, shaking its dusty feathers.

"That's right," Gabriel muttered. "Go away."

The bird didn't go away—but for the moment, at least, it seemed stymied.

Rue, who was squatting on a branch several feet above them, called out suddenly. "Hey!" She pointed away to the west. "Gabriel, can you see that?"

"Don't tell me it's another one," Gabriel said, and he followed the line of Rue's pointing finger to a gap in the foliage some distance off. At the far edge of the gap, perhaps a quarter of a mile away, was a large humped green shape almost completely obscured by vines and brush. Not another bird, that was for sure. It looked like . . . metal?

"What is it?" Gabriel asked, squinting.

"Tell me that's not a propeller," Rue said.

In the shadow of the green metal Gabriel spotted a large, paddlelike blade.

"No, that's a propeller, all right," Gabriel said.

"Which means a plane," Rue said, gleefully. "And that means a way out of here."

"But then . . . other people besides my father must have been here before us," Velda said.

"A long time ago," Gabriel said. "Judging by how old that propeller looks."

"I wonder what happened to them?" Velda said.

As if in answer to the question the giant bird suddenly reared up again and slammed its head into the trunk of the tree. Unprepared for the jolt, Gabriel swayed and nearly fell off the branch, the Colt slipping from his grasp and tumbling to the ground. The bird pulled back and slammed into the tree again, and then a third time. With each blow, Gabriel could hear the trunk creak and splinter. The bird pulled back and looked up at them. Gabriel could've sworn he saw a malevolent smugness in its eyes, as if the creature knew it was only a matter of time before dinner would be served.

Once more, the bird smashed the tree, and this time the branch Velda had chosen for her perch snapped, sending her slipping and clutching at branches far too weak to support her weight. She smashed through the branches, plummeting toward the bird's gaping beak.

Gabriel cried out wordlessly and sprang forward, laying his body out flat on his own sturdy tree limb and reaching down to grab Velda's forearm as she fell.

He caught her. She hung from his hand with her feet dangling, swinging like a tempting lure just inches above the gore-drenched beak below.

"Gabriel!" Velda cried. "Gabriel, I'm slipping!"

Gabriel tightened his grip further, feeling his fingertips sink bruisingly into her flesh, but her arm was slick with sweat and she *was* slipping, her arm sliding down along Gabriel's like someone trying to slip out of a pair of handcuffs. In another second, he'd lose her, unless he grabbed hold with his other hand—but he couldn't do that without letting go of his grip on the tree, in which case they'd both fall. Unless he could hold onto the limb with his legs alone—

Suddenly the bird let out a bloodcurdling scream as a spear flew out of the thick underbrush and stabbed deep into one of its eyes.

Gabriel looked back the way the spear had come. To his amazement, a young woman burst from a cluster of thick ferns. A second and a third, and then a half dozen more.

Each woman carried a spear, except for the first, who'd already thrown hers. They looked alike as sisters, each with dirty blonde hair and pale blue eyes, each tawny and young, nubile, their deeply tanned, honey-colored skin and lithe bodies glossy with sweat from the exertion of the hunt. They were dressed, if you could call it that, in scraps of black-and-tan-striped fur that had previously clothed a Tasmanian tiger less lucky than the brood Gabriel's team had so recently encountered.

While Gabriel hooked his legs around the branch and used both hands to haul Velda back up to safety, the hunters leapt onto the floundering beast, jabbing it with spears and beating it with stone clubs. Gabriel watched speechless as the huge bird finally collapsed, shuddered and died.

With the beast slain at their feet, the women's eyes all turned upward, toward the three people in the tree.

Chapter 16

Looking down, Gabriel saw one pair of women break off and go to work on the downed bird, efficiently gutting it, cutting it into manageable chunks, and wrapping the butchered pieces in stiff brown barkcloth. One of the women spent a moment combing through the contents of the butchered bird's stomach; Gabriel glanced away when he realized one of the discolored lumps he was looking at was the back of Nils's head.

The rest of the women split into two groups, one surrounding the tree where Gabriel, Velda and Rue crouched, the other going across the way to the tree Millie had climbed.

One woman bent down and picked up Gabriel's fallen Colt, examining it with great curiosity. Another began to gather up the scattered packs and bundles, poking at their contents as if the packs, too, were entrails to be sorted through.

"What should we do?" Velda whispered.

"Well," Gabriel replied. "They don't look overtly hostile."

"They've got spears and clubs," Rue said. "How much more overt do you get?"

"They saved our lives," Gabriel reminded her. After a moment, he said, "I'm going down."

He lowered himself slowly, avoiding any sudden movements. When he reached the bottom the women crowded in closer, spears in hand. They didn't raise the weapons, however. Rather, they reached out to touch him with their free hands, their palms and fingers traveling over his face and body without any trace of shyness.

"Hello," he said. "Thank you for what you did. We are very grateful." He tried this out in several languages—English, French, Chinese, Russian—but he didn't see the faintest glimmer of comprehension. Throughout, the women continued reaching out to touch, to probe, as though trying to figure out just what sort of creature he might be. "Ladies, if I might—"

One of them said something to him in a melodic, unfamiliar language and took him by the wrist, started pulling him toward the road. He limped after her, one foot clad only in a thermal sock. He saw his fallen boot resting at the base of a nearby tree and broke away to get it. "If you'll excuse me—"

Two of the women raised their spears in his path, crossing them in front of his face. "My boot," Gabriel said. "For my foot. Over there." He pointed, first at the boot, then at his foot, and then at the boot again. They didn't seem to understand the words, but his gestures were clear enough and finally the women raised their spears and let him through. The boot was slimy with the bird's foul-smelling saliva. When he sat down to pull it on, the women resumed their exploration of his body, one of them tugging at his hair as he bent forward, another lifting the collar of his shirt to peer inside.

Gabriel stood again and—as gently as he could—disengaged from the probing hands.

He looked back at the tree where Velda and Rue still sat, hidden among the branches. "Well, I don't think they want to *hurt* us," Gabriel said.

"That's good enough for me," Millie said, and he dropped down from his tree with a crash. The huntresses who'd been waiting at the base of the tree drew closer in a tight circle around him and began subjecting him to much the same scrutiny that Gabriel had endured.

"All right," Rue said. "Let 'em pick over me. Just as long as they get us to that plane."

But when she climbed down with Velda close behind, Gabriel realized just how wrong he was about the mysterious huntresses. Rue and Velda were instantly surrounded by spear points. One of the blonde women snaked a bronzed arm around Rue's throat and pressed the blade of a stone knife up under her chin.

"Don't!" Gabriel cried, palms out. "Wait . . ."

Another blonde grabbed Gabriel's wrists. He shook off her grip, but the woman with the knife at Rue's throat pressed it harder against her skin, drawing blood. She said something in the melodic tongue, which suddenly didn't sound very friendly at all.

The one who'd grabbed at his wrists seized them again, and this time Gabriel let her. He felt his hands being bound tightly behind his back and the empty holster being unbuckled from around his waist. He could have resisted, could have fought—but not with a knife at Rue's throat. He saw that Millie, too, was being bound, with a double length of thick rope at his wrists and ankles. They tied Gabriel's ankles as well, and then roped his to Millie's, linking them like members of a chain gang. Velda and Rue were bound together in a similar fashion, after which the women gathered up the meat and the scattered gear and then prodded their captives at spear point to urge them forward along the path.

"Not overtly hostile," Rue grumbled under her breath, and the woman beside her gave her a jab in the shoulder with the tip of her spear.

"Things could be worse," Gabriel said.

"How do you figure that?" Millie said.

"They could've killed us already," Gabriel said. "They must want us alive for some reason." Then he got a jab in the shoulder himself and shut up.

Gabriel could smell wood smoke. A pulsing beat of distant drums seemed to beckon them onward as they padded before their silent captors through the humid jungle. Clearly they were heading for some kind of encampment or village. Gabriel tried to crane his neck backward to make sure Velda and Rue were all right, but his own personal guard, a tall, leggy specimen with her hair pulled back in a tight, beaded knot, used the flat of her spear's blade to turn his face back to the trail ahead. Again, Gabriel took some comfort from the gesture. She might have used the point.

Several minutes later, they took a right-hand fork in the path and shortly arrived at a clearing in the jungle. The clearing was filled with round, thatched huts arranged around a single larger structure at the center that towered over the others. Its woven bark walls and high, slanting roof were extensively decorated with pictograms and colorful patterns of dots not unlike native Australian art. Surrounding the massive triangular door was an arch composed of skulls. The one at the peak clearly came from the same species of massive bird that had attacked the team. Also included were several toothy, long-jawed Tasmanian tiger skulls, a pair from what looked to be some kind of crocodile, and most disturbingly, a number of human skulls. The drumming stopped as they stepped into the clearing.

The entire population of the village, it seemed, came rushing out to marvel at them. Or more specifically at Gabriel and Millie. Rue and Velda were kept at the rear of the line and were utterly ignored other than by the huntresses standing guard beside them. All the town's inhabitants, though, clustered around Gabriel and Millie, jostling each other for a closer look. Strangely, they all seemed to be female, most ranging in age from what looked like their twenties to their fifties. There were also a handful of younger women, in their late teens perhaps, as well as two very old women who, though thinner and taller than most Australian aborigines, had similar facial features: dark eyes, dark skin imprinted with a variety of faded blue tattoos. Several of the older women had brown or reddish hair, but the younger ones more or less all fit the profile of the hunting party: blonde hair, blue eyes; full lips, proud noses; lithe builds, with long, muscular legs. Of the approximately two dozen women in the village, there was only one girl who looked preadolescent, a skinny child of eight or nine. Clearly their geographic isolation had resulted in severe inbreeding, and apparently not much breeding at all in the past decade. But then, Gabriel wondered, how *could* they be breeding at all? Where were the men?

One of the brown-haired women gave a command and the hunting party split in two. One half led Rue and Velda away toward the nearest hut while the other urged Gabriel and Millie around to the opposite side.

"I don't like this," Millie said.

"Try to keep an open mind," Gabriel said, but he

looked back at Velda's retreating figure with more than a little anxiety.

Their destination proved to be a small domed hut on the edge of the jungle, far from all the rest of the buildings. An anatomically detailed pictograph above the doorway made it clear that they were being taken to the men's quarters. Which at least answered one question: at least now they knew there *were* men's quarters. The tanned tiger-skin flap covering the door was lifted and the guards used their spears to prod the two of them into entering.

Once inside, Gabriel's nose was assaulted by a uniquely awful odor. Like a combination of burnt hair and rusted metal and bile. It was dark inside the hut except for a small, guttering fire in a shallow pit ringed by smooth river stones. It took his eyes several seconds to adjust to the gloom but when they did, he realized they were not alone.

Several figures were huddled on the far side of the hut. At first glance, Gabriel took them for children because of their size but once he'd gone up to them and looked more closely he realized that they were adults. All male and all suffering from some kind of wasting disease. They'd lost almost all their hair; few had more than a tooth or two in their withered jaws; and their bodies were shrunken and emaciated, like puppets built from sticks and paper. Their heads lolled on weak, scrawny necks and their sunken eyes peered at Gabriel and Millie hopelessly. A white-haired woman was squatting beside one of them and spooning some kind of steaming mush into his mouth.

"Jesus," Millie whispered. "What the hell is wrong with them?"

"I don't know," Gabriel replied.

"I sure hope it's not contagious," Millie said.

The old woman looked up at them, then set down her mush and picked up her sickly patient like he was made of feathers. She carried him into an area in the back, behind a woven partition, and then proceeded to do the same, one by one, with each of her other apathetic charges until Gabriel and Millie were alone by the fire.

The old woman departed without a word, leaving Millie and Gabriel to contemplate their situation.

Gabriel twisted his bound wrists, but found to his dismay that the slightest movement caused the rough bark rope to cinch tighter. It might be possible, though extremely difficult, for them to run with their hands tied and their ankles bound together—but how could they make it past the armed guards? And what about Rue and Velda?

"So," Millie said. "What do you think?"

"I don't," Gabriel replied. "Not yet. I was prepared to find all sorts of things up here—but not this."

"Well, while you're re-preparing," Millie said, "maybe we can find something sharp to use on these ropes. Maybe in that basket over there . . . ?"

"Worth a try," Gabriel said. "Ready?"

"Right," Millie said.

Together they moved across the room, taking only the tiny steps allowed by the rope that bound their ankles. They staggered together and apart, struggling to synch their steps so as to put the least amount of tension on the rope between them. It took them the better part of five minutes to make it to the lidded oval basket on the far side of the room.

"On three," Gabriel said. "One, two . . ."

They dropped to their knees in unison. Gabriel

leaned in and used an elbow to knock the lid off the basket.

Inside, there was a strange assortment of items. A pocket-sized Russian/English dictionary. A rusted compass. A tiny, battered doll with matted hair. A silver pocket watch with Hebrew letters engraved on the case.

"If we needed any more proof that we're not the first outsiders to stumble across this place," Gabriel said, "I think we just found it."

"Well, then, how come word's never gotten out?" Millie asked.

The two of them looked down at the heap of trinkets and neither spoke. They both knew the answer to Millie's question; it was obvious. Clearly the people who'd found this place before them hadn't made it out alive. Gabriel thought of the human skulls decorating the doorway to the building at the center of the village and felt a shudder course through him. He had to get the team out of this situation, and soon.

Millie rotated so he was facing away from the basket and bent backward, allowing his bound hands to reach the pile of objects. Gabriel watched as he dug through it. "Couldn't one of them have been carrying a Swiss Army Knife? A nail file, at least?"

"Nothing?" Gabriel said.

Millie came back upright, an object clutched in his hands—the pocket watch. Gabriel saw that the letters engraved on the case were a *chai*, the Hebrew word for life.

"This one's metal, at least. Maybe with the edge . . ."

Millie pressed the catch on the side with one thumbnail while Gabriel strained to bring his arms into reach. But Gabriel stopped straining when the cover of the watch swung open and he saw the black-and-white photograph on the inside. It showed a bearded man embracing a little girl with wild hair and a big smile. Gabriel knew that smile.

"It's Velda," Gabriel said. "This must have been her father's."

Gabriel bent as close as possible to read the faded handwriting at the bottom of the photo.

> *Happy 65th*
> *(the age when* other *fathers retire . . .)*
> *Love, Velda*

Gabriel told Millie what it said.

"Think he might still be alive?" Millie asked.

"If he were," Gabriel said, "I think he'd be in here with us."

Gabriel reached out to take the watch from Millie. Velda needed to see this—it might be as close as they'd get to fulfilling the purpose of their mission. Before he was able to slip it into one of the pouchlike pockets of his thermal briefs, though, the hide over the hut's entrance rose noisily and two young women appeared. He palmed the watch shut and closed his fist around it.

Chapter 17

The women who entered the hut carried bowls of hot water and armfuls of fragrant flowers and leaves whose strong aroma cut through the stench of sickness in the room, making it almost bearable.

They set the bowls down on either side of the fire, then pulled stone knives from crude sheaths at their hips. One approached Gabriel, the other Millie. The first said something—something Gabriel couldn't understand, of course, but he recognized the tone of warning in her voice. She raised the blade, brought it close to his chest. Out of a corner of his eye he saw the other woman doing the same to Millie.

"Count of three, boss?" Millie said under his breath.

"No," Gabriel said. "They wouldn't bring us here just to kill us."

The woman before him grabbed a fistful of his sleeveless shirt in her other hand.

"You sure?" Millie said.

"You remember what I told Velda about being sure?"

"You say lots of things, man. Hey—!" This as the woman in front of Millie grabbed a handful of his shirt as well, and no small amount of chest hair with it.

The woman brought her knife down in a swift stroke. The taut fabric beneath her hand sliced open.

With a similar stroke, the woman in front of Gabriel cut through his shirt as well.

They went around to the other side of the two men and Gabriel felt the torn fabric of his shirt being pulled back, away from his skin. The sound of two more slashes came—and it wasn't a shirt anymore, just strips of cloth that fell away to either side, leaving him still bound at the wrists but naked from the waist up.

The women came around again.

One of them spoke and gestured for them to stand.

"Now, look, sister, enough's enough," Millie said, but he stood as the sharp stone point came up under his chin, pricking not at all gently into his skin. Gabriel stood with him.

The stone knives made short work of the knee-length thermal underwear that was all they had left on other than their boots.

Without speaking another word, one of the women collected the other's knife and went to hand them off to someone on the other side of the tiger skin, while the other woman bent and came up with a double handful of the strong-smelling leaves that had been soaking in the steaming water. She began scrubbing them roughly up and down along Millie's torso, a look of intense application on her face.

The other woman returned, took a similar pile of leaves out of her bowl and slapped them wetly against Gabriel's chest. This close, the smell was overwhelming. But the herb-laden concoction was effective—Gabriel felt layers of caked-on sweat and grime coming off him as she washed.

He heard a swift intake of breath from Millie. "Lady,

you want to be gentle down there," he muttered. "Ah, hell, what am I talking for? She can't understand me."

Gabriel stifled an exclamation himself as the woman washing him reached the same delicate spot on his body. But she left it undamaged and moved on to his thighs and knees and shins.

"I don't know whether I'm being perfumed or prepared for a cooker," Millie said. The woman working on him had switched from water to a thick, scented oil, which she was spreading along his muscular arms with the side of a long feather.

Once they'd both been oiled from neck to knees, the women brought out a thick crimson paste and used it to daub spirals on their faces and chests.

Gabriel kept his fist closed tightly around the pocket watch and scanned the dark interior of the hut, inch by inch, looking for any weapon, any way to cut the ropes, any hope of escape. He found nothing.

When the women had the two men clean, oiled and decorated, they tied strips of painted barkcloth around their waists, forming a sort of short kilt of overlapping pieces. It was, Gabriel thought, just enough to maintain modesty—if you stood in a perfectly unmoving, upright position. He did.

One of the women clapped loudly and two others came into the hut bearing a platter of roasted meat. When Gabriel inhaled the savory aroma of the food he suddenly realized how hungry he was. The last time he'd eaten anything had been the chalky frozen energy bar. How long ago had that been? It felt like a different lifetime, a different world.

The women fed Gabriel and Millie by hand, tearing off long strips of meat that Gabriel suspected had come from their avian adversary and slipping them between

their captives' lips, keeping their fingers carefully outside biting range. Once the food was gone, the women
retreated, taking the empty platter with them. Gabriel
used the moment of privacy to lift his bound wrists
awkwardly and attach the chain of Dr. Silver's watch to
the waist of his kiltlike garment, tucking the watch itself underneath one of the barkcloth strips. It would
have to do.

He had barely completed this task when a quartet of
grim-faced huntresses appeared. One pair held Gabriel
and Millie at spear point while the other threw loops
of rope around their necks. They were led from the
hut, bound and leashed.

The reddish light filtering through the tinted ice above
seemed way too bright after the dim interior of the hut.
There was no hint of any kind of change to indicate the
passage of time. Was it night? Day? Down here there
was no way of knowing.

Their captors led them to the large central building,
through the skull-framed doorway and into a high-
ceilinged interior. Small basins of burning oil provided
flickering amber illumination that revealed more
painted pictographs swarming across the walls.

To the right was a row of steaming natural pools that
gave off a faint odor of sulfur beneath the heady mask-
ing scent provided by hundreds of white blossoms float-
ing on the water's surface. In the largest of the pools, a
group of women clustered around a single platinum-
haired bather who, at the sound of Millie and Gabriel's
arrival, slowly stood, water and petals sluicing from her
glistening nude form.

Her body, Gabriel noted with unwilling admiration,
was extraordinary. The flickering light and smoky shadows only served to highlight the trim musculature of her

arms and thighs, the taut abdomen below her strong rib cage, the fierce, proud breasts from whose engorged tips hung decorations made of polished bone. At the juncture of her thighs a slender curl of wet hair, as pale as the locks on her head, did little to cover her sex.

"Ah, hell," Millie said. "You can't dress me in a skirt and show me something like that." Glancing over, Gabriel saw the reason for his embarrassment. "Eyes front, boss," Millie said. "If you don't mind."

Gabriel watched as the woman's attendants, rising equally naked from the water behind her and climbing out onto the surrounding ledge, helped her into a flowing golden garment. It revealed more than it covered. Two of the attendants lowered an intricate woven headdress of flowers and bones upon her white-blonde head and, balancing it without any apparent effort, she slowly approached the two men.

Her face had a regal, almost aristocratic cast, though Gabriel couldn't say whether it was a matter of physical structure or just the way she held herself. Her eyes were the familiar pale blue, her features not measurably different from any of the huntresses they'd watched bring down the bird. She didn't even look as old as they did— she was twenty at most, more likely in her late teens— and she had a smaller frame. But her striking platinum hair set her apart from the others, as did her garment and headdress and bearing, and of course the deference all the others showed her. She was clearly the ruler of this village of women.

"Man," Millie said out of the corner of his mouth. "This just keeps getting more and more . . ."

"You are . . . English?" the woman said with a pale eyebrow arched. Gabriel and Millie exchanged a glance.

Her husky voice was flavored with some strange, unfamiliar accent, but the language she spoke was recognizable.

"American," Gabriel replied.

Her eyes narrowed at this bit of information.

"How is it that you speak our language?" Gabriel asked.

"My grandmother's grandfather teach to her many language. She teach to me," she said. "To me and to my sisters. I am Uta. I am Queen of Kahujiu."

"Uta," Gabriel repeated. "I am Gabriel Hunt. This is my friend Maximillian Ventrose. We came here to find another American who was lost near here—"

She waved dismissively.

"How many child do you make?" she asked.

Gabriel frowned. "I don't understand."

"Child," the queen said again, impatiently. "How many child do you have?"

"None," Gabriel said. "I don't have any children."

She turned to Millie.

"And you, do you make any chil . . . chil-dren?"

"No, ma'am," Millie replied. "None that I know of."

She scowled and spoke to her attendants in their native language.

"I have a bad feeling about this," Gabriel told Millie.

"Silence," the queen spat. "You do not speak together, only to me."

"Queen Uta," Gabriel said again, trying to keep his tone respectful. "We came here with two others, two women. Where are they? We would like to see them."

"The females are useless to me," the queen replied. She took a step closer to Gabriel and reached out to touch his painted chest. "*You* are useful. You and your friend." She looked over at Millie, not at his eyes or face, but at the very spot he'd asked Gabriel to politely look away from. A grimace curled one corner of her lush mouth and he heard her breathing quicken. Gabriel couldn't be sure in the amber light, but he thought Millie was blushing.

The queen returned her gaze to Gabriel, her expression once again sober. "Our tribe, we die. You understand? Our boy children. They begin strong, but grow weaker every year. They do not become men. Men who come here from beyond the sky can only make children for one-half of one cycle of light and darkness. After that, they too become weak and useless. It is the anger of the god Unterg that takes away their strength and their power to make children. You are strong, big. You last more than one-half cycle. You provide much seed, so our tribe live."

In Antarctica, half of one light and dark cycle would be six months. Gabriel had no intention of spending even another six hours in this village. He had to find some way out.

"But first, to settle roles, we have ritual," Uta said.

"What ritual?" Gabriel said.

"It is law: when more than one come from beyond the sky, they shall fight, prove who will make stronger children. The winner, he is mine. The loser, to the women of the tribe, each of them in turn." She looked over and down again, and this time Gabriel thought he saw her shiver slightly, perhaps thinking of her small frame and the prodigious instrument jutting between the plates of Millie's kilt. She took Gabriel's chin in her hands and leaned in close till her lips were nearly touching his.

"You," she said. "Fight hard."

Gabriel pulled his chin from her grasp. A flare of anger flashed across the queen's face. She gave a command to her guards and then turned away as Gabriel and Millie were led away by their rope leashes.

Chapter 18

Instead of being returned to the men's hut, Gabriel and Millie were brought around to the other side of the village. An enormous tree of some species Gabriel didn't recognize grew thick and twisted on the edge of the eucalyptus jungle and dangling from its heavy branches like huge wicker fruit were a cluster of spherical cages. The sight gave him a start—just a few months back, on a rescue mission to Borneo, he'd found the woman he was looking for in a cage suspended from a tree, about to be sacrificed by the remnants of an ancient Hittite cult. Now here were Velda and Rue, sitting hunched and apparently naked, each in her own tiny cage, unable to stand or stretch out their legs inside the woven spheres. A massive bonfire burned in a shallow pit nearby. The smoke was thick and black, making his eyes sting. It was not the sort of déjà vu he liked.

"Gabriel!" Velda cried, but one of the guards silenced her with a swift jab upward through the woven bars.

Two cages sat empty on the ground, their gates open. The guards sliced through the cord connecting Gabriel's ankles to Millie's and forced Gabriel at spear point to climb into one of the spheres. No amount of prodding and screaming was going to get Millie's massive frame into a four-foot-diameter cage, so as Gabriel was sealed inside his cage and hauled up using a heavy rope-and-pulley arrangement, the women resorted to lashing Millie securely to the trunk of the tree. Gabriel watched the process through the side of the cage. In their cages beside him, Rue and Velda were watching as well, he saw.

Giving the ropes connecting the cages to the tree one last going over to be sure they were secure, the guards left the team to dangle like aging meat.

Gabriel looked from side to side; Rue was on his left, Velda on his right.

"Thank God you're both okay," Gabriel said. "You are, aren't you?"

"We're alive," Rue said.

"They were pretty rough on us," Velda said. She turned one arm toward him to display a darkening bruise. "And they took our packs and clothes, and all our equipment." She nodded toward the large, smoky bonfire. "They burned everything."

"Now even if we could make it back up to the surface," Rue said, "we'd be dead of exposure in minutes."

"What did they do to you?" Velda said.

"Nothing good," Gabriel said. "Except clean us off. And they fed us a little," he admitted. "And gave us these loincloths."

"Hell of a lot better than the treatment we got," Rue said.

"Yeah, well, they're not looking to breed you."

"To breed—" Velda said.

Gabriel swiftly filled the women in on what had transpired: the sickly men, the queen and her demands, the ritual combat. When he finished, he fished the pocket watch out from under his kilt and, facing Rue, held it to a space between the bars of his cage. With one finger he flicked it open. He couldn't see Velda behind him, but he heard her sob.

"That's him," she said, her voice unsteady. "It's his. My god. I *gave* it to . . . Gabriel, do you think he's . . ."

"I don't know," Gabriel said firmly. "We didn't see him. All we know is that they had his watch." He replaced the watch under his kilt.

"Millie?" Gabriel called down. "Millie, how you holding up down there?"

"I got ants the size of my thumb using me for an expressway," Millie replied between clenched teeth. "So far no bites, but I'm gonna try to keep really still and not piss them off."

That was a smart plan for a nearly naked man tied to a tree that was crawling with ants. But a plan like that—keep still, do nothing, hope you don't piss off your enemies—was not one the group as a whole could afford to use.

Gabriel pushed his fingers through the weave of his cage and clenched his bound fists, pulling at the bars. Whatever kind of wood the cages were made of, it was both flexible and strong—it moved under his grip, but didn't break. He hissed with frustration and shifted his trapped and folded legs into a slightly less uncomfortable position.

Gabriel squinted through the bars at the red ice overhead. In the distance, he could see the thick shaft of white light pouring through the opening in the ice but could not see the opening itself.

"We've got to get over there," he said. "Somehow. Rue, if we made it to the plane, do you think you'd be able to pilot it through that opening?"

"Are you kidding?" Rue replied. "I can pilot a 747 through a hula hoop."

Rue sounded as cocky and confident as ever, but Gabriel could hear a brittle undertone of fear in her voice. And it only made sense. From the little they'd seen of the plane, it had looked like a vintage number, possibly from the 1960s, maybe older. Even if it were still functional after all this time and still had fuel—two very big ifs—depending on the exact make and model of the plane, Rue could have as little as twelve inches of clearance to make it out through that narrow opening. It would be a difficult enough stunt in a modern plane in mint condition with modern navigation tools. Who knew what sort of condition this plane would be in? Always assuming, of course, that they managed to get to it at all.

"We'll wait till they take us out for the ritual," Gabriel said. "If they want us to fight, they'll presumably give us weapons. Even if they want us to fight barehanded, at least they'll have to untie us first. That'll be our chance to rush them. We should be able to grab a spear or two at least."

"They'll be expecting it," Rue said. "They'll be on their guard."

"These are twenty-year-old women," Gabriel said. "Between Millie and me—"

"Don't underestimate them," Velda snapped. "They're seasoned, coordinated fighters—you saw how they took down the bird that killed Nils. You and Millie weren't able to do that. And there are dozens of them and only two of you."

"There are four of us," Rue said. "Unless you're too frightened to fight, princess."

"No, Rue," Gabriel said. "If you get free, I don't want you wasting any time getting involved with the fighting. First chance you get, you run. You understand?

You run as fast as you can and you get to that plane. We're all stuck here for good otherwise. Getting to that plane and getting it running has to be your top priority. And if you succeed—if you manage to get it up and running—and you don't see any sign that we're on our way—" Gabriel's voice trailed off. "We'll try to make it. I promise. But if we don't, you get the hell out of here and don't look back. You hear me? Get out and get back to safety."

"I won't do it, Gabriel," Rue said softly. "I won't leave you here."

"Well, let's hope you won't have to," Gabriel said. The emotion in Rue's voice touched him. Maybe she still had some feelings for him after all. "But if you have to, you do it. Someone has to survive to tell the world about this place."

A sound of footsteps from below indicated that the guards had returned.

Gabriel craned his neck to see what was happening. He could hear Millie swearing, and the women speaking to him in the local tongue, and then Gabriel saw Millie being led off by his leash.

Seconds later, he felt his own cage shudder and sway and then begin to lower.

Chapter 19

As the guards led Gabriel though the village, all the inhabitants turned out again, lining the pathways between the huts, tagging along behind Gabriel or reaching out to touch him as he passed. When they arrived in the center of the village, several women were hauling aside a heavy woven mat about ten feet in diameter. Beneath the mat was a stone-lined pit. Gabriel couldn't see the bottom, but he could hear Millie's angry voice coming up from below.

The guards slung a rope under Gabriel's arms and used it to lower him into the pit, dropping him the last six feet to the hard-packed dirt floor. Millie hurried over as the women up at the top yanked the rope away.

"You okay?"

"Dandy," Gabriel replied, getting to his feet again and taking stock of his new surroundings.

The pit was approximately twenty-five feet deep, damp and claustrophobic. There was a bad smell, like fear-sweat and spoiled meat. The stones of the pit walls were slick and mostly featureless except for what looked like some kind of asymmetrical drainage hole, about a foot wide, off to one side. Even in the dim light, Gabriel couldn't help but notice the brown stains of dried blood on the stones surrounding it.

A shout came from above and something was slowly lowered on a rope: a stone knife, the rope looped through a hole in its broad handle. A second rope followed, with another blade. When they had descended enough for Gabriel and Millie to grasp them in their bound hands, the men set to work sawing through the ropes around their wrists. Gabriel freed his hands and bent to cut his ankles free as well, but before he could, the rope from which the knife hung was abruptly yanked upward and the knife shot out of his grasp, slicing his palm on its way up.

Gabriel raised his gaze and saw that Millie had also had the knife wrenched from his grasp. Gabriel wiped his bloody palm on his barkcloth kilt and began working on the knots at his ankles. He saw Millie doing the same.

"Christ," Millie said when he finally kicked the rope off. "Now what?"

Gabriel looked up. The walls were too steep and slick to climb. "Even if I stood on your shoulders, it still wouldn't get us out of here," he said.

"You will fight," said the voice of Queen Uta from above.

Gabriel saw the queen's face peering over the edge. Her platinum hair was piled up into a complex braided coif.

"The man who cannot get up is the loser," Queen Uta said. "The winner will make royal daughter to be my heir. The loser will be given to my sisters. To make more daughters. There is much work to be done before jealous Unterg takes away your manhood.

"You shall not kill," Uta continued, "and you shall

not harm the organs of generation. Failure to observe this rule shall be punished by your most slow and painful death."

"What if we refuse to fight?" Gabriel called up.

"You *must* fight. It is the law." Uta's voice sounded more puzzled than angry.

"And if we don't?"

She thought it over. "You shall be punished," she said, "by your most slow and painful—"

"Death, right. No, I don't think so," Gabriel said. "That would deprive you of our seed. If it's true that your tribe is dying, killing us would be like killing yourselves."

There was no response to this. Queen Uta's face vanished, and the silence went on long enough that Gabriel started to think they'd been abandoned in the pit. Perhaps that would be their punishment: a slow death of starvation at the bottom of this crude oubliette.

Then he heard a clamor up above, the sound of something being dragged to the pit's edge. Two new faces appeared: Rue's and Velda's. They were lying facedown, their throats pressed against the ground, a fist tangled tightly in each woman's hair.

"You fight," Uta's voice resumed, as though there had been no interruption, "or your *women* die a slow and painful death."

"Ah, hell," Millie muttered.

Gabriel saw several women come into view around the perimeter of the pit, Uta among them. They looked down eagerly, expectantly. Impatiently.

He bent forward in a grappler's stance. Millie bent forward to match. When their faces drew close, Gabriel whispered, "New plan. We put on a good show for them, I win, and then when I get her majesty there alone, I should be able to overpower her. Once we have her, we should be able to control her subjects."

"There's just two problems with that plan, boss," Millie said. "To start, you're assuming they'll let you be alone with her. More likely, they've got some sort of ritual for getting the queen pregnant that involves all her handmaidens standing around with spears pointed at your ass."

"I'll take that chance," Gabriel said. "What's the other problem?"

"No offense," Millie said, "but nobody in their right mind is gonna believe that you could win a fight against me down here."

"Why, Millie," Gabriel said, "I'm surprised at you. It's not like you to get a swelled head."

Millie shrugged. "Just stating the facts. Up on a castle wall somewhere, with swords or guns or ropes to swing from, there's no one better than you. But down here, with nothing but our fists and no room for anything fancy? I'm just saying, Gabriel. It's not plausible."

"Well, that's why you'd better make it look good," Gabriel said, and threw a punch at Millie's jaw. The big man took it without flinching, then after a second remembered and jerked his head back.

"Work on your timing," Gabriel whispered.

"Sorry," Millie said.

"Now you throw one."

"I don't—"

"Do it."

Millie cocked back a big fist and let Gabriel have it. Gabriel staggered backward, clutching a bleeding nose. The crowd above howled bloodthirstily.

"Damn it," Gabriel muttered, struggling to shake off the effects of the blow. "Not *that* good."

Millie shrugged. "Sorry," he said again.

Gabriel moved cautiously to his right and Millie mirrored him, circling. Gabriel spoke low, between clenched teeth. "Play it like you're big but slow. That will buy us a little time, at least."

Millie nodded and took a couple of wide, bearlike swipes at Gabriel who danced back out of his reach. Millie raised his foot to kick Gabriel in the knee and Gabriel took two swift and agile steps up the stone, pushing off and landing behind Millie as the big man's foot slammed into the wall above the drainage hole. A cascade of dust and grit sifted down from between the bloodstained stones. Millie limped backward, selling the pain in his leg like it was the Brooklyn Bridge.

Gabriel leapt onto Millie from behind, clinging to his back and Millie slammed him backward against the wall.

"I'm gonna throw you," Millie said. "You ready?"

"No," Gabriel said. "But go ahead."

Before Gabriel could catch his breath, Millie peeled him off and tossed him through the air. He landed hard against the opposite wall and slid down. Seconds later, Millie grabbed Gabriel by his shoulders and hauled him back to his feet.

"You ever watch pro wrestling when you were a kid?" Millie whispered.

"Not so much," Gabriel said, swinging at the side of Millie's head. The big man jerked under the impact more convincingly this time. "But my sense was those guys used a padded mat."

"Not always," Millie said, and flung him across the pit, where he crashed into the wall above the drainage hole for the second time. Gabriel felt the impact in his spine. He also felt one of the stones in the wall shift behind him, knocked loose by the successive impacts. He was struck with a sudden idea.

He lunged back at Millie and wrapped an arm around his neck, pulling Millie's ear down close.

"Throw me against the wall by that hole again," Gabriel whispered. "As hard as you can."

Millie did as instructed and Gabriel felt the loose stone shift again. One more blow and it might come free.

"Throw a kick," Gabriel whispered. "Use the same leg as before and really play up that you're hurt."

"Got it," Millie said.

He swung wide with a stiff kick, missing Gabriel by a mile and knocking the loose stone out of the wall. Gabriel threw a kick of his own, striking Millie in his supposedly injured leg. Millie howled and went down on one knee. The loose stone was about the size and shape of a cobblestone, and it was heavy when Gabriel hefted it.

Millie was right: the women wouldn't believe that Gabriel could best a man of Millie's size and strength bare-handed. And if the women thought they were shamming, they might well take it out on Rue and Velda.

"Sorry, Millie," he whispered, positioning himself so his body was blocking the queen's view. "I owe you an aspirin." And he brought the stone down, the muscles in his arms wrenching tight as he checked his swing just before connecting. The stone still hit, with a crack that carried all the way back up to where the women were waiting to hear it. Millie dropped as if he'd been shot.

Gabriel let the stone fall to the ground and raised his arms, breathing heavily. Were they cheering up there? It sounded like it. Then he saw something raining down on his upturned face. Flower petals. He turned back to where Millie lay, crumpled and unmoving. He was struck with the sudden fear that maybe he really had hurt his friend. He dropped to a crouch beside him. There wasn't any blood that he could see, but—

Millie's eyes cracked open narrowly. "Just like the pros," he whispered, and grinned. He closed his eyes again.

Gabriel felt a flood of relief as he stood again. But it was short-lived. An instant later, he felt a sharp jab in his chest, like a nasty hornet sting. His fingers flew to the source of the pain and found a colorful feathered dart protruding from his left pectoral muscle. He pulled the dart out and flung it away but before it hit the ground, the world around him went liquid and untrustworthy. Black and red shapes swirled around him and he unceremoniously followed the dart to the floor.

Chapter 20

Consciousness came to Gabriel in stages, like a shadowy striptease. First there was an awareness of a sound, a nearly subliminal hum just above the very bottom range of his hearing. Then a hazy sense of firelight flickering through his closed eyelids. A lush, sultry aroma not unlike crushed frangipani; and underneath the cloak of sweetness, an odor distressingly sharp and electrical, like ozone. Gabriel stirred, tried to stretch but couldn't. When he opened his eyes, he discovered he was bound naked and spread-eagled on a pile of furs. Each limb was tied to a thick stake driven deep into the dirt floor, allowing perhaps a three-inch range of movement in his arms and only slightly more in his legs. Off to his right and level with his chest, there was a fifth stake, but instead of anchoring a part of his body, this stake was tied to a rope stretching straight up and across the dim, distant ceiling.

Gabriel strained and stretched his neck, evaluating his surroundings. As he appeared to be in a high-ceilinged room, it had to be another chamber inside the large central building—nothing else in the village was nearly that tall. By craning his neck, he could just make out, behind him, a triangular doorway draped with tanned skins. Past his feet, a pit of glowing coals burned sullenly in the center of the room, raising the already high temperature, and past that was an odd wooden structure. An enormous tree trunk had been split in half and the halves—each the size of a good-sized canoe—hollowed out to form two long chutes that were propped up in a steep V-shape on a wooden scaffold. The rope tied to the fifth stake approached the chutes across the ceiling and then branched when it got to them, one end running down the middle of each. Above this, a large circular hole in the ceiling let in a shaft of reddish light. Whatever lay beneath the shaft of light, where the angled chutes intersected, was hidden behind an elaborately woven screen decorated with more of the white blossoms that had rained down on Gabriel in the pit and decorated the queen's bath. Whoever owned the floral concession around here was making out like a bandit, Gabriel thought.

Movement at the top of the chutes drew Gabriel's eye and he squinted, trying to make out what was going on. The rope was twitching, almost as if it were attached to something inside the chutes that was squirming or struggling to get out.

He turned back at the sound of footsteps behind him. Queen Uta stood beside his head, towering over him with her strong legs planted wide and her fists clenched. She had on a minimal outfit of fur, one strip across her breasts and a minimally broader one around her waist. Her platinum hair had been brushed loose, flowing nearly to her hips.

"I see that you are awake, Gabriel Hunt," she said. "And that you are prepared to perform your sacred duty."

Gabriel was mortified to find that she was right.

Even tied down as he was and with no shortage of other things on his mind, Gabriel was responding to the sight of her sleek, oiled and barely dressed body much as Millie had when they'd first encountered her. He wished he had on at least the few strips of bark-cloth their captors had allowed them then, to conceal his reaction, but the stripped-off kilt lay in a pile by his feet.

"I'd be better able to perform my sacred duty," he said, "if I weren't tied up like this. Why not at least re-lease one of my hands? Wouldn't you like me to touch you?"

She smiled and crouched down beside him, caressing his bare chest.

"Yes, Gabriel Hunt, I would like you to touch me," she said. "But I cannot free your hands, not even one, because I cannot be sure that would be how you would use it."

"Are you afraid I will hurt you?" Gabriel said.

"Hurt me?" She shook her head. "This is not my worry. I cannot allow you to kill yourself, not before you give me a child." She slid a slim stone knife out from a strap of leather she wore around one leg. She set it on the floor beside the fifth stake.

"Kill myself?" Gabriel frowned at the knife. "Why would I do that?"

"It is a shame that you cannot ask your predecessor, Dr. Silver, this question." She leaned in close. "But I am afraid his answer died with him."

Gabriel felt a cold elevator plunge in his gut. From the far side of the room, he heard an anguished, muffled cry and then a rhythmic pounding, as of a fist beating against a wooden door. He looked toward the scaffold-ing with its V-shaped construction on top and saw that the right-hand chute was rocking. And even muffled, he recognized the voice.

Velda.

"What have you done with her?" Gabriel said. The left-hand chute showed signs of movement as well. "Are they both here? The women who came with me?"

The queen stood, her eyes narrowing.

"Why do you care?" she asked. "Were they your lovers?"

"They're members of my team," Gabriel said. "I'm responsible for them. Like you are for your people."

"You are responsible for them no more," she said. "They are in their place and have their duty. You have responsibility for only one woman now." She ran her hands up over her glistening golden flanks and taut belly.

The muffled shouts grew louder on the far side of the room.

"Your women are blessed," the queen said. "They have the privilege to become brides of Unterg. Their sacrifice assures a strong healthy daughter." She reached out to touch the fifth rope. "At the exact moment when the seed of child is put into my body, I cut this rope. The brides go to their destiny, and my daughter comes into hers."

"What destiny?" Gabriel said, his throat constricting as he spoke.

"Unterg is a jealous god," the queen said. "We must make him satisfied or he will give me a sick son instead of a strong daughter."

Gabriel strained against the ropes holding him down. "You can't do this," he said. "I won't let you."

"Enough," Uta said. "It is time. First, we ask the blessings of my ancestors."

She stepped out of Gabriel's sight for a moment and returned with a woven basket in her arms. Setting it down, she drew from its depths an intricate oval head-dress studded with crimson feathers and carnivore teeth that looked razor sharp. She placed it reverently on her head. "We must both wear the sacred objects of my ancestors. This is the crown of my grandmother's grandmother. And for you, the crown of my grandfather's grandfather." She bent over the basket again. As she did this, Gabriel turned his attention to the stone knife lying on the dirt floor. It was a good six inches out of his grasp. He struggled to reach it, all the muscles in his arm stretching to their limit, but there was no way.

The queen turned back, a flat, dark cap of some sort held between her hands. This was no primitive construction of tooth and bone and feathers—it was a man's hat, somewhat battered and faded. From the back, it looked like it had once been part of a military uniform. "My grandfather's grandfather was the first father of our tribe. You have a great honor, Gabriel Hunt, to wear his articles."

She bent over him and set the cap on his head, then stood to admire it. Gabriel shook it off onto the ground beside him and saw her face twist with anger. "You will wear it," she said in a tone of cold command. "You will not cast it off!"

Gabriel turned his head, curious to see if he could figure out where the cap originally came from. Maybe whoever had flown that ancient plane . . . ?

His jaw dropped open in speechless astonishment when he saw the tarnished metal insignia above the black patent leather bill.

An eagle.

Clutching a swastika between its claws.

Chapter 21

Queen Uta snatched the Nazi cap up off the ground and cradled it to her chest. She brushed it off gently and replaced it on Gabriel's head, pulling it down firmly so the fit was tight. Then she strode purposefully across the room to the woven screen. "You will obey me," she said. "You will obey, or your people will suffer the wrath of Unterg."

She reached out and folded back the screen.

At the base of the two wooden chutes a spidery, jointed metal framework held up a round machine shaped like a fat, riveted steel onion. A verdigris-covered nozzle protruded from the bottom while above the top of the machine a giant concave lens perhaps six feet in diameter was suspended in metal clamps. The space between the lens and the top of the device seemed to shimmer and crawl with distorted waves like heat coming off summer asphalt. Looking at the shimmer made Gabriel's eyes ache and his head throb almost instantly.

The hum that had been buzzing softly in Gabriel's ears since he came to was louder now.

And at the base of the two wooden chutes, trussed hand and foot and gagged, were Rue and Velda, each woman struggling furiously against her bonds. The chutes were angled directly at the shimmering space under the lens and would have deposited them there if it hadn't been for the rope descending from the ceiling and looped tightly around their wrists.

The machine was giving off a pulsing red glow that amplified the reddish light coming down from above.

Across its side, the metal onion bore the same stiff-winged eagle-and-swastika design as the military cap Gabriel had on. Slightly off center beneath the Nazi insignia were faint red letters: UNTERG. To the right of these letters, Gabriel could barely make out the ghost of three more, faded nearly to invisibility. An A . . . what might have been an N . . . and the last nothing but a fragment of a curve that could have belonged to an O, a C or a G. If you didn't speak German, you might puzzle over the word, but Gabriel did speak German and had no difficulty guessing what it had been. *Untergang.* It was a word with several meanings, none of them good.

Ruin. Extinction. Doom.

"Witness," the queen said, "Unterg's power."

She picked up a loose stone from the ground and carefully threw it into the shimmering space between the lens and the top of the machine. There was a blinding flash and the ozone smell sharpened until it was almost overwhelming. The stone was gone without a trace. Velda began to shout again behind her gag, and this time Rue joined her.

"Let them go," Gabriel said, struggling but unable to get free.

The queen shook her head. "They must be given to Unterg," she said. "It is the only way to assure a healthy daughter."

"But you said if I *didn't* obey my people would feel

Unterg's wrath—now you're saying they'll be given to Unterg even if I *do* obey."

"Oh," Uta said, "I did not mean these two. I meant your *people*. You are American, you said. Is it not so? I meant I will spare the people of America—for a time—if you obey. If not . . ."

She turned a dial on a control panel at the base of the machine, near the nozzle. A metal cover slid open and Gabriel saw an old-fashioned display flip through a series of numerals with a loud clatter, like a mechanical sign in a train station. The whirling digits finally came to a stop and Gabriel strained to read them from across the room.

3853N7702W

Coordinates—38 degrees, 53 minutes North, 77 degrees, 02 minutes West.

The coordinates for Washington, D.C.

The nozzle at the base of the machine dropped an additional six inches with a loud clank, exposing a boxlike section at its base. A black button ringed with red protruded from its side.

"Through the earth's core," Uta said, "through the belly of your land and up from beneath, Unterg's power will stream death upon your people. It was for this—to establish Unterg's throne, and from it to stab at the depraved and greedy heart of America—that the first fathers came to this land some sixty-six cycles past." A downcast look came over her face. "But Unterg took our fathers, one by one, before they could complete their task. When the last among them lay dying, he passed his duty to his queen. She passed it to my grandmother, who passed it to my mother, and my mother passed it to me, as I will pass it to my daughter and she to hers: to trigger Unterg's wrath when the command comes from afar, from Defuror, Unterg's emissary on earth."

Gabriel winced. "Der Fuehrer," he said.

"Yes," Uta said, "Defuror. We are to await his instruction—as we have awaited it with patience and reverence and humility for cycle upon cycle, generation upon generation. We are told to wait, and we wait; we are prepared to wait until the end of time. Unless," she said pointedly, "a queen shall have no heir. In this event, the last queen must trigger Unterg's wrath before she passes. And a queen may so trigger it sooner, if she believes her breeding of an heir is at stake." She tapped the black button gently with a forefinger. "I shall, Gabriel Hunt. I shall trigger it, if you refuse to give me a daughter. I shall trigger it before your eyes and a thousand times a thousand of your kinsmen shall die, their blood upon your head."

Gabriel tried to picture Lawrence Silver lying where Gabriel lay now, a frightened old man, a survivor of the camps, held prisoner once more by captors in Nazi regalia, being forced into complicity with a murderous plan left over from the Third Reich. With no prospect for escape, no way of knowing his daughter was on her way with help. Gabriel could understand why, when the opportunity arose, the man had seized it and chosen to end his life.

Gabriel would be given no such opportunity.

The queen came forward, walking slowly toward where he lay. "I shall do all this," she said, "all these deeds of blood and calamity, I shall reave your world till none are left to cry for mercy; with no remorse shall I do these things, unless you give me what I require."

She lifted one hand to her hip and drew open the

knot holding the fur wrap closed around her waist. It fell to the ground, leaving her bare beneath. Then she did the same with the fur top she wore, releasing her heavy breasts. The decorations of polished bone had been removed and in their place, hanging from the points of her engorged nipples, were circlets of tarnished metal. As she came closer, Gabriel recognized them as the lightning-bolt epaulets from an SS uniform.

"You will give me my heir now," she said. Planting one foot solidly on either side of his torso, she lowered herself to her knees, straddling him. She leaned forward, her breasts hanging above his chest. The warm metal of the SS insignia scraped across Gabriel's skin. Then he felt the wet length of the queen's tongue run along his neck and the underside of his chin.

She reached behind her and took him in her fist. He bucked forcefully with his hips, arching upward, but she held on, squeezing hard with her knees against his sides like a bull rider. He twisted and bucked again, and this time she fell forward against him, chest to chest, her face landing next to his. "You are strong," she said. "And vital." Her voice rose exultantly. "You have more fight in you than the old man. And more of *this*—" She reached back and took hold of him again, in a grip that was almost painful. Perhaps it was the adrenaline, perhaps the feel of her lithe young body pressed against his, but he was, to his dismay, miraculously still tumescent.

She reared up, raised herself half a foot in the air using her knees for leverage, and plunged down, taking him deep inside her. "Now," she said, "you shall fill me with your strong, vital American seed."

He watched her lift the stone knife from where it lay beside the fifth stake. He strained to resist the climax he felt building in him. But it was hopeless. She held him clenched tight with muscles as thoroughly developed as those of her powerful arms and legs; he felt them squeeze rhythmically as she rocked upon him.

She threw her arms wide and he saw the blade stroke against the taut rope, fibers parting as it passed. He shot a glance over her shoulder, toward where Rue hung by her wrists in one chute and in the other, Velda—

But Velda wasn't in the other.

The rope that had held her wrists dangled empty.

Had that one swipe of the blade been enough to release her into the maw of the machine? But no—he'd have heard it if she'd fallen, would have smelled the ozone stench.

"Now, Gabriel Hunt!" the queen shouted, raising the knife with one hand and pressing down on his belly with the other. "Now!"

And she would have gotten what she wanted, had not a pair of hands hauled her off him by the throat at that very instant.

The queen's headdress tumbled from her head as Velda hurled her to the ground.

For just a moment, Velda locked eyes with Gabriel. He saw the depths of pain in them, the inconsolable rage contorting her features. "Get me loose," he said quickly. "We have to free Rue before that rope breaks." A glance to the side showed that the rope was fraying rapidly, the twined strands snapping one by one as fewer and fewer remained to bear her weight.

But Velda didn't look at the rope or stoop to untie him. She strode the other way, away from Gabriel and toward Uta.

The queen was trying to rise to her knees. "That old

man," Velda growled, her voice low and savage, "was my *father*." Velda laid her out with a vicious kick to the throat. Then she drew back her leg for another, but the queen snagged her ankle and pulled her down to the ground.

"Rue," Gabriel called. "Hold on!" He strained to reach the fallen headdress, which lay on its side just inches from his right hand. He could feel the tip of one of the crimson feathers between his fingers. It took three tries before he was able to get a good enough grip on it to draw the headdress toward him, one slow millimeter at a time.

But eventually he had it—and rotating it between his fingers, he brought one of the sharp teeth with which the headdress was studded into contact with the rope. He began sawing.

As he did, Velda and Uta rolled past, clutched tightly in each other's arms, both of them sweat-streaked and dirty and naked as the wild animals their struggle made them resemble. Gabriel saw Velda grab a fistful of platinum hair, wrenching it hard to the left; he was surprised Uta's neck didn't snap from the force. But it didn't, and the queen responded by streaking a long-nailed hand across Velda's throat, which erupted in furrows of blood.

Velda raised Uta two feet in the air with a kick to the stomach that sent the queen sprawling. An instant later, she was up again and slashing at Velda with the stone knife. Velda leapt back, out of the blade's reach— and at that instant, the last knot around Gabriel's right wrist parted. He swung his arm over and began tugging at the knots around his left. They had tightened from his struggles, but he could feel them begin to come apart as he worked at them.

He shot a glance at Rue and then at the dwindling rope holding her up. She was trying to wedge herself in the chute using her knees and heels, but it wasn't working—she kept slipping. And her efforts were making the rope part faster. "Stay still," Gabriel shouted. "I'm coming."

He saw Velda throw a punch at the queen. Uta dodged, twisting out of the way and bringing the knife up to slash at Velda's knuckles. Velda hissed and jumped back, shaking blood from her hand. She came back in with a low kick and the queen responded again with the knife, this time slashing at Velda's calf. Velda swore, feinted right and then slipped in on the left, catching the queen by the wrist and disarming her with a brutal twist against the natural bend of the joint. The knife dropped from her grip.

Velda made a dive for the fallen knife and the queen instantly fell on her from behind, knocking Velda to the floor. She wrapped her legs around Velda's chest, pinning Velda's arms to her sides, then took hold of Velda's hair and began bashing her face into the dirt. Velda managed to wrench one arm free and elbowed the queen in the kidney. She made another grab for the knife, but the queen brought her fist down, hard, on Velda's wrist. Velda howled with pain.

Both women staggered to their knees, then unsteadily to their feet, but the queen lurched forward, butting Velda in the back with her head. Velda fell, landing at the edge of the fire pit. The queen dropped to the ground beside her, taking a fistful of hair and forcing her face toward the smoldering coals. Velda threw back a flurry of desperate elbows until finally one connected, knocking the queen to one side, but Uta came barreling back and shoved Velda onto the coals. Velda rolled across the burning surface, sending sparks flying. The queen spun, reaching for the fallen knife.

That was when Gabriel finally got his left arm free—and the last strands of the rope holding Rue up snapped.

With a lightning-fast lunge, Gabriel swung over toward the stake, grabbing at the rope as it sprang into the air. He caught its end and held tight. Rue's weight yanked him to a standing position as she slid down the chute. He heard her moan when her feet came to a stop within inches of the deadly lens. Pulling hard with both hands, he dragged the rope toward him, coiling it around his fists. The muscles of his arms bulged with the effort. One more pull—

As Rue reached the top of the chute, her weight toppled the wooden scaffold, sending her sprawling on the ground.

The sound caught Uta's attention and she looked over. As she did, Velda grabbed her from behind, wrapping one arm tightly around her throat and pressing fiercely against the back of her head with the heel of her other hand. The queen's face began to go purple. She was struggling for breath.

"Velda, no!" Gabriel shouted. He raced to undo the ropes around his ankles. "You'll kill her!"

Velda looked over at him. When she spoke, it was with utter disgust in her voice. "So?" she said, and shoved hard with the hand at the back of Uta's skull. They all heard the queen's neck break.

The struggling body went limp in Velda's arms.

She carried it to the doorway and shoved it through. Moments later, armed guards began pouring in, spears held high. A robed, older woman came in behind them,

Uta's corpse held in her arms, its head lolling horribly. "Who," she said, her voice halting, her accent heavy, "who . . . does this?"

For a tense moment, no one moved or spoke. Then Velda stepped forward, eyes blazing. "*I* did it."

The woman holding Uta's body lowered it to the ground and went down on one knee. One by one, each of the other women did the same. A low, rhythmic chant swept through the crowd.

The older woman spoke again. Gabriel couldn't understand the words, but their meaning became apparent when the woman took the oval feather headdress from where it lay on the ground and went over to place it on Velda's head.

Chapter 22

"I am Anika," the woman said to Velda. "Sister of . . . greatmother . . . of Uta. I have only small English, but I . . . serve you now, my queen."

"Your queen," Velda said.

"Yes," Anika said.

Velda shook her head, almost as though trying to clear her ears. "Leave me. Now."

"My queen?"

"Now," Velda said. "Get out." She pointed to Gabriel. "I wish to be alone with the man. To complete the ritual that Uta began. Leave us."

Anika nodded and translated to the others. The villagers did as their new queen ordered and as soon as they were gone, Velda grabbed the stone knife and handed it to Gabriel. He made short work of the ropes around his ankles and then limped over to where Rue still lay, bound and gagged.

When she was free, Rue reached up and took the Nazi cap off his head. He hadn't remembered he still had it on. She scaled it into a corner of the room. "You look better without that particular piece of clothing. Though we'll need to get you some somewhere."

"You, too," Gabriel said. "Both of you." There was

an uncomfortable moment as they all looked at each other, naked as the day they were born, the old lover and the new, and the man they'd both shared.

And the newest lover, lying dead at their feet.

Velda went to where Gabriel's kilt lay and picked it up. She handed it to him, unlatching her father's pocket watch from it first. As Gabriel tied the kilt around his waist, Velda looped the watch chain around her bloody throat, wearing it like a necklace. She opened the watch and stared at the photo inside until tears began to run down her smeared cheeks.

Gabriel went over to her, tried to put his arms around her, but she pushed him away.

"They killed him," she spat. "They finally killed him."

"She said he killed himself," Gabriel said. "Maybe he saw no way out. Under the circumstances . . ."

"They killed him!" Velda shouted. "They murdered him, just like they always wanted to. And they'll pay for it."

"I don't think they wanted him dead," Gabriel said. "And Uta at least has already paid as much as she's ever going to." He nodded toward the body.

"Uta?" Velda said. "You think I'm talking about *Uta*?" She pushed the body over with her foot so it was facedown in the dirt. "She was nothing. A tool, manipulated by the men who built this machine." Velda walked over to the steel device on its metal frame, looked with unfettered loathing on the eagle and the hateful symbol in its claws. She spat on it, and her saliva ran down the center of the swastika.

"*They* were the ones who tried to kill him. Sixty years ago they tried. But he beat them. He survived. They killed his entire family—every relative he had, every single one. His own brother, younger than him, a little child, they killed. Shot in the head. But they didn't manage to kill my father. Oh, no. He was strong; he lived. And every day he lived was a repudiation of them and everything they tried to do, it was a . . ." She slapped the side of the machine. It rang like a bell, a low tolling sound. "It was a goddamn miracle. A victory over those bastards, every single goddamn day. But now . . . They finally got him. They got him, and they killed him. And they're going to pay for it."

"You can't make someone pay," Gabriel said quietly, "who's been dead more than half a century."

"Of course you can," Velda said, her voice burning like acid. "Of course you can. You can make them pay by destroying what *they* cared about, what *they* loved. Their precious Fatherland, their blessed Aryan people. Two world wars because of those sons of bitches, millions of people killed, and now my *father*, tied down and raped by this Nazi whore—" Velda's chest was heaving. She crouched beside the machine, looking at the dial Uta had turned. She spun it, and the coordinates went clattering to new settings.

"What are you doing?" Gabriel said.

"What do you think," Velda said.

"You can't set off that machine," Gabriel said.

"I can't? *I can't?* Who do you think you're talking to, Hunt?" She stood. "It's *my* machine now, isn't that what they said? I'm their queen and it's my machine to use any way I want!"

"Velda, come on," Gabriel said, "I know you're angry, but—"

"*Angry? Angry?*" She realized she was shouting and lowered her voice. It was, Gabriel thought with horror, even more frightening when she spoke quietly. "I am not *angry*, Gabriel. I am merely . . . vengeful. I'm sure the coordinates for Berlin can be programmed in there somehow. Wonderfully appropriate, don't you think? That the descendants of the men responsible for my father's death will . . ." Her voice caught, and then she smiled, terribly. "Will feel . . . Unterg's wrath."

Gabriel stepped forward, but Velda shouted, "Anika! Guards! Come quick!" A half dozen women charged into the room, spears at the ready.

"Take them," Velda said, and the women did, one pair grabbing Gabriel's arms, another Rue's.

"What do you . . . wish to do . . . at these?" Anika said, haltingly.

Velda thought for a moment. "Put the man back in that pit where he was before," she said. "I'm sorry, Gabriel. But I have to. I can't let you interfere."

"Woman too?" Anika said.

"No," Velda said. "No, not the woman. Rue, you are going to get that plane running again. So we can get out of this godforsaken hellhole."

"You really think I'd help you?" Rue said.

"If you don't want your boyfriend there to stay in that pit till he dies of starvation," Velda said, "I do think so, yes. And you don't really want to stay here any more than I do, do you?"

"You're crazy, lady. Completely batshit insane."

"Rue, Rue, your language," Velda said. "There are young women present." Then to Anika: "Take her away. To the plane in the jungle."

"Plane?" Anika repeated with a quizzical expression.

"The thing that brought your, your mother's grand-father or whatever the hell it was . . . the thing that brought the men here from the world above," Velda said. "The first men."

"Ah, the Father Bird," Anika said, nodding.

"The Father Bird," Velda said. "There you go. Take her to the Father Bird, give her whatever tools or help she asks for—but if she refuses to work or tries to escape . . . kill her."

"If you kill me, you're stuck here," Rue said, twisting to get out of the guards' grip. It didn't work.

"You think you're the only one who knows anything about airplanes, little Rue? I've flown a few in my day myself," Velda said.

"From nineteen-fucking-forty-four?" Rue said. "Through a narrow hole in a sheet of ice?" Velda didn't answer and Rue nodded with satisfaction. "You need me, and you know it."

"Maybe so," Velda said. "But you only need to be *alive* to fly the plane. You don't need to be whole. Anika?" The older woman nodded. "Tell the guards to cut off her toes if she disobeys or causes any trouble. Start with the smallest toe on her left foot, then the next, and so on. If you run out of toes, let me know and we can start on Gabriel's. That'll make her work."

"Yes, my queen," Anika said, her face ashen but obedient. She translated the instructions and the guards began dragging Rue off.

"Are you out of your mind?" Rue shouted as they dragged her away. "What's gotten into you?"

"Velda, please," Gabriel said. "Please, think about what you're doing."

"I have thought about it," Velda said. "And it makes me very happy." She motioned to Anika. "Take him away. And . . ." She looked down at her nude and filthy body. "And bring some water. And something decent to wear."

She turned her back on Gabriel. The guard to his

right stuffed a wad of sour-tasting leather into his mouth and strapped it in place with a hank of thick bark rope. Gabriel let out a sound of anger and frustration, but the gag reduced it to a muffled grunt. Surrounded by spear points, Gabriel was led out of the ritual chamber and away from Kahujiu's new queen.

Outside, Gabriel was marched across the clearing to the pit where he had fought Millie. Where the hell was the big man anyway? Still doing his duty with the other women of the tribe? Looking around, Gabriel could see no sign of him anywhere. But he didn't have time to wonder for long before being prodded over the edge.

He turned in midair as he fell and managed to land on his feet, rolling backward and slapping his arms out to either side to dissipate the impact; even so, the jolt from the twenty-five-foot drop was still painful. He sat up as the pain slowly subsided. The pit was just as he'd left it, except that the loose stone he'd used to clobber Millie was gone. The murky half-light, the awful smell, the damp chill, all unchanged. The mossy stone walls just as impossible to climb.

Gabriel fought to remain calm. To think. He had to find a way out, a way to save Rue and stop Velda. There had to be one. But how?

Chapter 23

Gabriel's thoughts circled helplessly in his head as he paced the perimeter of the pit. He still felt there had to be a way out—but if there was, he'd made no progress toward finding it.

He had made several failed attempts at scaling the slippery walls, jamming his fingers and toes into the narrow mossy cracks between the stones. Each time he'd barely gotten six or seven feet up before losing his grip. If only he had some basic climbing gear—even a pair of sturdy sticks that he could jam into those cracks and use as handles, like peg climbing back in high school gym class. But there was nothing, not a branch, not a bone.

He was about to try again with his bare hands when he heard a sound from above. The flat, dragging sound of something heavy sliding across the dirt at the edge of the pit. He looked up just in time to see his circular view of the crimson sky blotted out by a bulky shape. Someone else was being shoved into the pit—someone large.

Gabriel hadn't met too many people that size, and as far as he knew there was only one in this village at the moment. He bent his knees, braced himself against one wall, and did his best to cushion Millie's fall, taking some of the impact against his chest and letting the big man roll off onto the ground in a heap.

Nursing his bruised ribs, Gabriel went to where Millie lay, sprawled on his side, moaning softly. He still wore the kiltlike getup but it was now quite disheveled, several of the barkcloth slats missing, and the paint on his body was smeared and mostly rubbed away. Gabriel could see one of the feathered knockout darts protruding from Millie's neck just below his right ear.

"Millie," Gabriel said, pulling the dart out and tossing it aside. He rubbed the big man's wrists and slapped his cheeks. "Millie, are you all right?"

No response. At least he was breathing normally and seemed uninjured beyond the various scrapes and bruises sustained on the way down—but there would be no waking him until the drug wore off.

It took the better part of an hour for this to happen, and when it did Gabriel was clinging to the wall some eight feet off the ground, desperately trying for a higher handhold and failing to secure one. He heard a groan from below and let go, dropping to the ground.

Millie groaned again, turning his head from side to side. He moved his hands to touch his neck, feeling for the now absent dart. Then finally his eyelids slowly peeled open, his blurry gaze struggling to focus on Gabriel.

"Christ," Millie said. "I thought . . ."

He made a move to roll over and let out a roar of pain. When he rolled, he revealed the leg that had previously been folded beneath him. His ankle was turned at an angle that it wasn't meant to go.

"Don't move," Gabriel said. "Your ankle's broken."

"Yeah, I noticed," Millie said. He was starting to

sweat profusely, his face pale. "Damn it, I go to sleep in the arms of three beautiful women and I wake up with you and a broken leg. What the hell happened?"

Gabriel quickly filled Millie in on everything that had taken place from the moment they had been separated.

"Their new queen?" Millie said. "You're kidding, right?"

"Wish I were," Gabriel said. "Here, sit up." He helped Millie to a sitting position, leaning against one wall of the pit. He reached for the waistband of Millie's kilt.

"Whoa, slow down there, boss," Millie said. "Just because we're in this hole together with time to kill—"

"Don't flatter yourself," Gabriel said. "There's nothing else down here to splint your ankle with, and we're not getting out of here if you can't walk."

"Why can't we use your kilt?"

"Yours is bigger," Gabriel said.

"Well, as long as you admit it," Millie said, forcing a pained smile. "All right, boss. Do what you've got to do."

Gabriel untied the big man's kilt, layered the stiff strips of barkcloth on either side of the fractured bone, and cinched the leather waistband tightly around them. Millie grimaced as he pulled the knots snug. "How's that?"

Millie tested it, gingerly at first and then with more confidence—though he leaned heavily on Gabriel's shoulder as he did. "Bad. I won't be clog dancing for a while. But I should be able to hold myself upright."

"That's something, anyway," Gabriel said, looking around once more. He thought about the offhand comment he'd made the first time they'd been down here, about standing on Millie's shoulders. Between them they totaled nearly thirteen feet; with his arms outstretched over his head, call it fourteen and a bit. Add the eight feet of free-climbing he'd managed at his most successful and you only got to twenty-two feet—close, but still well short of the top. And that was assuming Millie's splinted ankle could support not only the big man's own weight but Gabriel's hundred eighty pounds on top of it.

Fine. If they couldn't go up, how about down? Gabriel bent to the task of inspecting the ground at the bottom of the pit, peering closely at every crevice and declivity in the dirt.

"What in god's name are you doing?"

"Wasting precious time," Gabriel said as he completed the survey. He stood up and worked the circulation back into his cramped thighs. "But I had to try. Last time I needed to get out of an underground trap, there was a secret tunnel with a hidden entrance you could barely see unless you knew it was there."

"Boss, if you're looking for a tunnel down here, you don't need to go searching so hard," Millie said. "There's one right there." And he pointed toward the drainage hole.

Gabriel looked at it. The opening was much too narrow for either man to fit through—but Millie was right, there was presumably a tunnel of some sort behind it. The villagers would sluice water down into the pit to wash away blood that had collected, along with other detritus, and the water had to come out somewhere, maybe in the stream they'd seen near the waterfall.

Could the channel behind this opening be wider than the opening itself? If they'd had to dig it without modern boring tools, it would have been easier to make it wider—specifically, the width of the person doing the digging—rather than narrower.

He bent to look at the space where the stone they'd knocked out used to be. On the other side he didn't see more stone, he just saw blackness.

"I don't suppose you could kick out any more of those stones," Gabriel said.

"Not with this foot," Millie said, slapping one thigh. "But with the other . . . ? I could give it the old college try."

He lay on his back, taking all pressure off his broken ankle, then aimed the tough, calloused sole of his other foot at the wall. He slammed it home. The first kick didn't do much—but by the time he'd dealt out a half dozen thunderous blows, another stone was coming loose. Gabriel dug around its edges with his fingers and pried the heavy block of stone free. He laid it on the ground.

"More," he said.

In all, they managed to remove four stones before Millie let his leg drop and lay back, exhausted. "I'm shot," he said. "That enough?"

The hole was wider now—just wide enough, Gabriel thought, to admit his broad shoulders. No way Millie could fit, but one person would be enough. If he made it out, he could come back for Millie. "I'm going in," Gabriel said.

"You sure?"

"Didn't we go over that already?" Gabriel said. He squeezed into the opening before Millie could respond.

Inside, it was dark, except for the slight glow of bio-luminescent moss faintly outlining the walls. It was narrow, too, the stone ceiling no more than two feet above the damp dirt floor. And it looked like it got narrower as it went—the people who'd dug it had presumably been young women, not six-foot-tall men. But maybe if he hunched down and was willing to lose a bit of skin on his shoulders—

He cocked his head. There was a low scrabbling sound coming from the darkness in front of him, like the scratching of claws. Animals of some sort—scavengers, perhaps. Then he heard a louder sound: a thumping, as of a paw, or perhaps a tail, batting against the ground.

He reached ahead of him with one hand, sweeping it back and forth along the dirt. He felt the air stir as something darted out of the path of his arm.

His fingers brushed along something hard lying half-buried in the ground. A bone? He grabbed it, wrenched it out of the dirt—and as he did, he felt a pair of sharp teeth sink into the flesh of his arm.

He swung the arm up and against the tunnel wall beside him, heard a squeal as the animal released its hold and dropped off. But the clattering of claws was louder now, and it sounded like it was all around him, as though the animals were somehow emerging from the walls of the tunnel itself. A furry flank slammed against the side of his face and he felt sharp claws scrape across his cheek. Another animal leapt over his shoulder and bit down hard on the back of his neck.

"Millie! Get me out of he—" His open mouth was suddenly filled with warm and greasy fur. He felt it wriggling back and forth and realized the narrow squirming thing probing inside his mouth was an animal's head. He bit down hard and spat the thing out just as he felt a pair of strong hands clamp down on his ankles and forcefully pull him out of the tunnel.

He emerged into the light with Millie on his knees beside him. The big man hauled two of the animals off his back and slammed their heads together, then threw them aside. Gabriel himself took care of the one clinging to his throat, knocking it off with the thing in his hand—which did turn out to be a bone: a scraped-clean femur that looked distressingly human.

Gabriel swept the bone along his chest and legs, knocking more of the animals to the ground. But more still were pouring out of the drainage hole, maybe attracted by their fellows' distress, or maybe just by the prospect of fresh meat.

The creatures looked like a cross between shrews and rats, only larger than any of either Gabriel had ever seen. Each was more than a foot long and had a pair of sharp prognathic tusks protruding from below an elongated snout. And they were more aggressive than any rats he'd encountered, even in New York, jumping on him and Millie with no regard for their own safety, no fear.

Gabriel batted them away as they came, while Millie fell back against one wall and did the best he could while balancing on his good leg.

"Jesus Christ," Millie said, picking one off his thigh before it could make the leap it was attempting onto his unprotected crotch. "What *are* these things?"

Whatever they were, a dozen more were boiling out of the hole in the wall. They were all over Gabriel in an instant, screeching, clawing and biting even as Gabriel swung and kicked out blindly in all directions. As soon as he got hold of one to smash it against the pit wall, three others seemed to take its place. The hot, musky stench of the creatures was nearly unbearable and their sharp teeth and claws were everywhere he turned, tearing into his flesh. In the frenzy, he lost track of Millie but he could hear him somewhere behind him, shouting and flinging the furry attackers aside.

"We've got to block up that hole," Gabriel said, dropping to his knees by one of the large blocks of stone they'd so painstakingly moved aside. He hauled it up in both arms as one of the animals leaped over the stone and onto the back of his hand. With a grunt, Gabriel pressed the stone into place at the bottom of the drainage hole. It did little to stop the flow of angry shrews—they just kept coming.

"Get over here, damn it," Gabriel shouted, plucking a shrew off his upper arm, where it had begun to make a meal of his triceps. Out of the corner of his eye, he saw Millie lumber over and bend to lift another of the stone blocks. He shoved it on top of the one Gabriel had placed. Gabriel himself lifted the third of the stones and jammed it into place as soon as Millie's hands were out of the way, and then Millie was there with the fourth.

The fit was far from airtight—hell, it wasn't even shrew-tight, as evidenced by the continuing appearance of furry snouts between the stones. But the fit was tight enough to be a squeeze for any but the skinniest of the animals and the constant flow subsided, enabling Gabriel to pick off the ones that remained in the pit, first two or three at a time and then one by one as their numbers dropped. Millie, meanwhile, grabbed up bodies of fallen shrews by the fistful and shoved them into the spaces between the stones like so much fleshy mortar.

"Sweet Jesus," Millie said, finally, lowering himself exhaustedly to a patch of ground from which he'd swept a layer of bloody animal corpses. Gabriel sat beside him, sore all over from bites and scratches and the bruises and abrasions he'd sustained in bashing the creatures against the rock. He felt weak and wanted desperately to lie down and sleep, even just for a little bit. But he knew that with the sun beating down and nothing to eat or drink, he'd only feel weaker when he woke—assuming he didn't find himself waking with more of the animals somehow chewing on his jugular.

Getting up, he kicked aside the bodies before him and bent to retrieve the bone he'd taken out of the tunnel. It *was* human, the leg bone of some previous visitor unfortunate enough to find himself fighting for his life in this pit. Well, it was too late to do the bone's original owner any good—but he might be able to do them some.

Gabriel handed the bone to Millie, who turned it over in his hands and looked up at Gabriel quizzically. "Can you break it?" Gabriel said. "Two pieces, equal length would be best."

"You don't ask for much, do you," Millie said. He took one end of the bone in each hand, then thought better of it and reset his grip closer to the center.

"Careful," Gabriel said.

"Why do you want a broken bone?" Millie asked.

"I don't," Gabriel said. "I want a pair of titanium climbing pegs. But I'll settle for a broken bone."

Millie gripped tighter, the veins standing out along his thick forearms. The bone bent in a narrow arc, then a bit farther, and then snapped in two, one piece just slightly longer than the other. He held the pieces out to Gabriel, who looked at the angled edges where the bone had broken. Nice and sharp—but all the same, he began working them back and forth against the face of one of the rougher stones, like a knife against a whetstone. The bones needed to go in smooth and come out the same way, and penetrate as deeply as possible into the cracks between the stones, and that meant taking off any rough edges or protrusions and sharpening them even more.

Gabriel kept at it for what felt like an hour, though he knew it probably was less—it was hard to tell much about the passage of time here. The reddish light streaming down from above remained unchanging, and the only sound was the scrape of bone against rock.

Gabriel wondered what he would find when he finally hauled himself up over the rim of the pit. What if he was too late? Velda might have figured out how to set the coordinates, in which case Berlin might be gone, or all of Germany—who knew what sort of devastation the Nazi doomsday device might be capable of. Or, of course, the machine might no longer work properly after sixty-five years, and might casually destroy the wrong country. Perhaps it had been locked on Washington for so long it would be impossible to redirect it, and when Velda pushed the button . . .

He shook his head. He couldn't let himself think about it. He had to clear his mind of everything but the climb. One thing at a time, and right now the one thing that mattered was getting out of this pit.

When Gabriel finally had the bone pieces as sharp and smooth as he wanted, he stood, stretching his arms and shoulders. He felt the pull and sting of every cut and bruise. His calf throbbed where it had been clenched in the unclean jaws of one of the biggest of the shrews, a long-fanged monster that had been murder to pry loose. It was going to be a tough climb and he was hardly in the best shape for it. But what choice was there? He took in a deep breath, stepped forward, and sank one of the bones into the highest crack he could reach.

Chapter 24

Raising his feet off the ground, Gabriel swung by the arm holding the bone wedged into the wall. At the top of the swing, he reached up and planted the second piece of bone about six inches higher than the first. Hauling himself up on the second piece, he pulled the first piece free and swung up to plant it higher. Then he repeated the process. Again and again he pulled out the bones and drove them in higher, sometimes as much as a foot above his previous handhold and other times only a few inches. There were times when he failed to drive the end of the bone into the wall at all and swung back away, returning a moment later for another attempt. His arms were already aching although he'd barely climbed five feet, but he kept on going, scanning the rock wall for cracks and crevices that might admit the bones—and that would hold his weight.

By the time he had made it halfway up the sheer face, his arms and chest were trembling from the effort and he was barely able to pull himself up inch by excruciating inch. Only thoughts of Millie waiting below with his broken ankle and Rue being forced at spear point to work on the plane—and Velda, half mad with grief, with the lives of millions in her hands—kept Gabriel pressing on. He didn't look down and barely looked up, concentrating instead on the wall directly in front of him: the next crack, the next handhold. Twelve feet became fifteen; fifteen became twenty. He was less than three feet from the lip when the stones supporting his latest handhold began to crumble.

It began with a faint rain of grit and dirt on his arm; then the terrible feeling of the bone in his hand coming loose. The stone below his fist had a crack running down its face, and as he watched it slowly widened.

Desperately, Gabriel swung the bone in his other hand and jabbed it into the wall just as he lost his grip on the first. It slipped from his hand and plummeted end over end to the bottom of the pit. As he swung reflexively out of the way of a small avalanche of stones, he heard Millie's voice from far below. "You okay?"

"I've been better," Gabriel called back. He held tight to the one remaining bone. This one remained embedded, but at a bad angle—tilted slightly downward and looking as if it were seconds from coming loose.

He looked up. He was close—so close. But still more than an arm's length away. He planted his toes against the rock, scrabbling for any sort of hold at all, and swung his free arm up. It caught nothing. No handhold, nothing to grab onto.

He tried again, aiming this time for the crumbling ledge where the stones had come loose. It was dodgy at best, unlikely to support his weight for long, but it was the best hope he had.

He reached it, caught hold. His fingers bit down fiercely, clamping onto the stone. It did feel loose, unstable—but he held tight and shifted until he felt the balance settle, and when it felt about as good as it was likely to get, Gabriel yanked the sole remaining bone free.

He swung by his fingertips twenty-three feet above the ground, holding onto this unsteady bit of rock, his heart racing. He could picture Millie looking up at him, holding his breath in fear, maybe holding his arms out to catch him if he fell, though the impact would surely shatter the already fractured bones of his ankle, maybe crippling him for life.

There was a happy prospect—Millie walking with a cane for the rest of his life, and all because of him. Gabriel forced the image out of his mind and swung his arm up, up, as high as he could, and stabbed the bone savagely into the space beneath one of the stones at the pit's edge. He didn't let himself swing back. Instead, he clenched the muscles of his abdomen and with an enormous effort swung his legs up. For an instant he hung sideways, like a gymnast on a pommel horse, then he managed to hook one ankle over the lip. He paused for breath in that awkward, stretched out position and then carefully worked his knee up over the edge, then got his other leg up beside the first. It took almost as great an effort to unlock his grip from around the bone clenched tightly in his fist, but he did, and wrenched himself up and over till he was lying flat on his back, looking up at the underside of the crimson dome of ice.

For several seconds, all he could do was lie there and breathe, trying to bring his heartbeat back down to something resembling its normal pace and hoping no one decided to show up and jam a spear into him while he lay there gasping like a gaffed bass. He slowly rolled over and raised himself to his hands and knees, adrenaline pulsing in his aching limbs and readying him for yet another fight. But nothing happened. There weren't any guards around, only two old women and one young girl, the one he'd seen when they'd entered the village; she sat alone, working on stringing a long necklace of seedpods and bone beads. The two old women sat side by side about ten feet away from her, next to what looked like a crude well, and were concentrating on grinding some sort of wild grain. One was cracking open the thick outer husks and placing the softer grains into a hole in the ground while the other was lifting and dropping a heavy wooden post to crush the grains to flour. None of the three were paying any attention to him. Gabriel was about to slip away and quietly hunt for something that might help him get Millie out of the pit, but the sight of the old woman cracking the husks made him do a double take. The implement she was using—it was the butt of a gun. Not just any gun, either. Gabriel's Colt.

"Hey!" he said. All three of the women looked up at the specter before them, a nearly naked man covered with rock dust and streaks of mud and angry red scrapes and swollen bite marks. The two older women fled like startled pigeons, the wooden post and gun left lying where they'd fallen from their hands.

The young girl stood unmoving, gaping at him wide-eyed. The paralysis was only momentary, though. When Gabriel took a step toward her, open hands held out in a nonthreatening display, she bolted, too, leaving him alone in the center of the village.

Where was everyone else? Were they all guarding Rue? Or were some in the tall central building, watching unwittingly while Velda turned their god machine against innocents in their ancestors' homeland?

Gabriel walked over to the primitive grain mill and

picked up his Colt. It didn't seem obviously worse for wear, other than a dusty coating of cracked hull fragments clinging to the grip. It was an antique that had once belonged to one of the Old West lawmen, either Wyatt Earp or Bat Masterson; it had been through worse. He brushed it off and slipped it under the waistband of his bark kilt. The gun wasn't loaded, but its familiar weight still felt reassuring.

The structure next to the grain mill was indeed a well, and Gabriel swiftly hauled up the large hollow gourd that served as a bucket, greedily sucking down massive gulps of the cold, clean water. Then he filled the gourd again and untied the sturdy rope from the wooden post from which it hung. He brought the gourd to the edge of the pit and set it down while he anchored the rope to one of the support poles of a nearby hut. The rope was damp but seemed flexible and strong. He hoped it would hold Millie's considerable weight.

"Hey, Millie," he called, lifting the water-filled gourd and carefully lowering it into the pit. "Room service."

Gabriel saw Millie pull himself up on his good leg and reach for the lowering gourd. When it landed in his hands, he drank deeply, emptying it in a single gulp.

"Damn," he said. "It ain't Abita, but it'll do." He gripped the rope and gave it an experimental yank. "This anchored?"

"Yes," Gabriel said. "Do you need me to rig some kind of pulley system to get you up or do you think you can make the climb?"

"My arms ain't broke," he replied and immediately started climbing, fist over massive fist.

In thirty seconds, Millie was up, sitting on the lip of the pit, bathed in sweat, teeth clenched tight from his obvious pain.

"We've got a choice," Gabriel said. "We can go in there—" Gabriel nodded toward the tall central building "—and deal with Velda, or we can see if we can spot the plane first."

"You're the one who's always saying to have an escape route planned out before you go in somewhere," Millie said, wincing as he got to his feet.

"True enough." Gabriel walked to the tallest nearby tree. "You stay put, rest that ankle." He jumped and grabbed hold of a low-hanging branch, chinned himself on it and got one leg up and over. From there he was able to make his way up, a branch at a time, to the upper regions of the tree. When he neared the top, he could see the plane. It was in a slightly different location than the first time they'd seen it and was surrounded by what looked like nearly the entirety of the village's able-bodied population. Everyone wanted to see what Rue was doing with the Father Bird, apparently—or maybe all hands had been needed in order to move it.

Either way, the plane had been moved and uncovered; the encroaching vines and brush had been cleared away, revealing not just the plane but also a makeshift runway before it. The plane itself was a curious-looking antique, with far too many wheels along its belly and four huge propellers lined up in a row along the wings, two on either side of the cage-style cockpit. The long skinny tail ended in a broad, H-shaped fin that was decorated with a pair of black swastikas outlined in white. The body was battered and rusted but looked intact. Gabriel was pretty sure that he was looking at an Arado Ar 232 transport aircraft. Built to transport heavy cargo, including vehicles, it would have been an obvious choice to carry the bulky Untergang device. But why had a plane equipped with wheels rather than skis been chosen for an Antarctic mission? Could the Nazis have somehow known in advance about this warm tropical anomaly? How, when even modern satellite imaging had been unable to detect it? And if they had, why was there no record of the discovery found among Nazi papers at the war's end?

Gabriel had no answers to these questions. And he knew there was no time for pondering them, not now. The plane had been moved, the runway cleared. And as he watched, he saw two of the propellers cough into motion, slowly at first, then faster. A moment later, they cut out—but in Rue's hands they'd be going again, he knew that. And then the other two would. With Rue working on it, that plane was going to take off, with or without them on board.

And that meant there was no time to spare.

Chapter 25

"The good news," Gabriel said, "is that most of the village is over there, meaning there can't be more than a few people guarding Velda."

"From what you described," Millie said, "I'm not surprised. She's not gonna want a lot of witnesses to what she's up to—someone might figure out what she's doing and try to stop her."

"The bad news," Gabriel said, "is that I'm sure the ones she's kept around her—or, what may be more likely, the ones who refused to leave her side—are the diehards, the ones who'll fight the hardest to protect her."

"You really think they'll fight for Velda the way they did for Uta? They never even met her before a day ago."

"It's not Velda they're fighting for," Gabriel said. "It's the queen of Kahujiu."

Millie threw up his hands. "So what do you suggest, boss? We haven't got any spears, that gun of yours is empty—"

"They might not know that," Gabriel said.

"Maybe not the locals," Millie said. "But I'm pretty sure Velda can count to six."

Gabriel pulled it from his waistband anyway. "She might have forgotten."

"And I'm limping like Long John Silver. Won't be much help in a fight."

"Then we'll just have to try and take her without a fight, won't we?" Gabriel said, and stepped through the skull-framed archway, gun held high.

The first room they came to, with the pools and the flickering oil flames, was empty, the surface of the water in each pool still. They passed through to a short corridor and from there could see around the edge of a hanging animal hide into the room where Gabriel had been staked to the floor. The furs were still there, and the stakes, too, and the spherical machine at the far end atop its tall metal frame. Velda was crouched by its base, facing away from the doorway, peering at what looked like the yellowed pages of a notebook lying spread open on the ground. Anika stood beside her, waiting for a command, while two young huntresses, each gripping the wooden shaft of a spear in both hands, flanked them and kept an eye on the entrance.

Gabriel raised his left hand with three fingers extended, then silently curled one inward toward his palm. A second later he curled the next one in, leaving only his index finger sticking out. Millie nodded. Gabriel curled the last finger in. Sweeping the hide to one side, he burst through into the chamber and ran all out toward Velda, leveling his gun at her back. He heard Millie enter behind him and saw the eyes of the two guards widen as they saw him. Six foot seven, muscled like a stevedore, and completely naked except for the splint on his ankle, Millie would have widened the eyes of anyone who saw him coming toward them—but for these two young women, whose lifetime exposure to the male of the species had been limited to the sickly examples in the men's tent and more recently the elderly Dr. Silver, Millie must have been an imposing sight indeed. That didn't stop them from lowering their weapons and racing to block Gabriel's charge— but it did buy him a few seconds, and in that time he was able to cross half the room.

He tucked his head down and somersaulted past as one guard stabbed her spear at the spot where his chest had been. The other darted to intercept him, but he dodged around her and grabbed Velda as she rose to her feet. She was dressed in a crimson gownlike garment that crisscrossed over her barely covered breasts, wound around her slender waist and then flowed open to the ground behind her, revealing every inch of her tan, muscular legs. On her head was the feathered headdress.

Gabriel pulled her to him with one arm around her waist. With the other he pressed the barrel of the Colt to her temple. He held her, squirming, as a barrier between him and the guards, both of whom were making tentative stabs in the air with their spears, trying to find an opening that would let them get at him without injuring Velda. He kept angling and re-angling her body to prevent them from getting through, but one darted her blade past Velda's shoulder, driving it two inches into his. He jerked back, blood flowing down his arm.

"Tell them to drop the spears," Gabriel said to Anika, "or your new queen dies."

"Don't listen to him," Velda said. "That gun's got no bullets in it."

"It's got one," Gabriel said, "and one's enough."

"You're lying."

"You sure?" Gabriel said coldly and pressed the metal harder against her skull.

Velda didn't answer, but her squirming subsided.

"The spears," Gabriel said again. Anika said something to the other two in their native tongue, and the young women responded in kind, the tone this time less musical than martial. Gabriel pulled back the hammer of his gun, producing an unmistakable sound that instantly plunged everyone into silence. "The spears," Gabriel said.

With angry expressions, the women reluctantly bent to obey, laying their spears on the ground. Millie limped over and collected them. Gripping both spears point-upward in one hand, he leaned on them and breathed a sigh of relief. He hadn't only stripped them of their weapons; he'd gotten himself a decent walking stick in the bargain.

"Now, tell them to step away," Gabriel said, and Anika translated. The two huntresses shook their heads, said something angry in protest, but Anika insisted and they backed off. Not very far, though.

"Tell them to leave the building," Gabriel said. The protests were louder this time and the women refused to budge. "You take them," he told Anika. "Leave and take them with you."

Now it was Anika who protested, in her halting English. "I cannot . . . go. I needs remain with . . . queen. With Unterg."

"Velda," Gabriel said, "order her to go."

"You won't shoot me," Velda said, her courage returning as more time passed without Gabriel pulling the trigger. "Even if you do have a bullet left, you won't use it on me. I know you well enough to know that." And with a powerful twist of her torso that tore the thin fabric of her gown open, she wrenched herself free.

"Now!" she shouted, ducking and racing back toward the machine. "Get them!"

The two guards leapt forward, one toward Millie, who swung the pair of spears at her legs; the other at Gabriel, who sidestepped out of her path. The one attacking Millie jumped lightly over the spears as he swept them toward her. She rammed into him, overbalancing him and taking him down to the floor. But he turned as he fell and landed on her, his three hundred pounds pinning her to the ground. She clawed and kicked, but had no way to lift him off her. "Sorry, miss," Millie said gently, in his sonorous voice. "I sure hate to do this to you." And he brought his forehead down with a swift crack, smacking hard against her brow. She went out like a snuffed candle.

Gabriel, meanwhile, was circling with the other guard, their arms outstretched. She took swipes at his torso, raking him twice, her nails scraping painfully across his chest. He swung the Colt at her but she avoided it nimbly and came in under his arm with a head butt to the sternum. He staggered back a few paces and she followed relentlessly, flailing at him with punches that carried more force than her slight build would have led Gabriel to expect. He shoved her back and shot a glance over his shoulder. Velda was at the machine again, one hand on the dial that set the coordinates. Her other finger hovered near the black button.

"Damn it," he muttered, and he flipped the gun in his hand, reversing it so he was holding it by the barrel. He swung, feinting left and then bringing his arm down and up hard from under, catching the guard squarely beneath her chin. Her head snapped back, and her whole body went limp. Millie, who'd just made it back up to his knees, caught her as she fell and laid her on the ground beside the other guard.

"Go," Gabriel said to Anika, and this time the older woman didn't argue, just slipped out through the doorway, a frightened expression on her face.

Gabriel turned to face Velda. She was kneeling on the ground by the machine, the notebook in one hand. The numbers on the readout by the dial now said 5231N1317E.

The coordinates for Berlin.

"Don't do it," Gabriel shouted, launching himself toward her with one arm outstretched. He had a sudden image of himself barreling down the stone stairs in the castle in Transdniestria, Djordji by his side, Fiona Rush bound helpless at the knife thrower's mercy. That had been bad enough. This was worse—far worse. "Don't," he said again, reaching for her, a note of pleading in his voice. "Millions of people could die—"

"Good," Velda said, and pushed the button.

Chapter 26

"What have you done?" Gabriel said. Reaching Velda's side, he pushed her away from the machine, which had started to hum at a higher pitch. He felt a profound and terrible resonance in his bones and behind his eyes as the machine powered up. Pulsing, hot, angry red light was coming from an opening above the nozzle, and the shimmer beneath the lens had intensified, becoming excruciating to look at. Gabriel squinted and turned away. His temples were aching, the pain intensifying and fading in time to the machine's pulsing rhythm.

"Give me that," Gabriel said, snatching the notebook from Velda's grip. There was something written on the front in soft lead pencil, the lines faint with age but the slanted, precise penmanship unmistakably Teutonic.

UNTERGANG PROJEKT
Josef Groener, Ph.D.

The interior pages were covered with the same handwriting, along with a number of pen-and-ink drawings of the device and its internal workings. Behind Velda, against the far wall, he saw an open metal footlocker, presumably where she'd found the notebook, or from which Anika had retrieved it for her.

He flipped quickly through the pages. "How do you turn it off?"

"You can't," Velda said, her voice suddenly drained of all energy and emotion. "This Dr. Groener, he's very, very clear about that. Once the button is pressed . . ." She waved a hand in the air. "You cannot shut it off."

"There must be a cutoff—"

"None," Velda said. "These were men who took destruction seriously. No going back."

He whipped furiously through the remaining pages, translating snatches as he went.

To target Washington, device must be placed at precisely the following coordinates, any deviation will reduce intensity in inverse proportion to the square of the distance . . .

Internal batteries shall concentrate energy of southern sun but shall not exceed nine hundred kilojoules; any excess to be released in the form of ambient radiation . . .

And this, underlined heavily at the bottom of a page: *Of paramount importance, please note, once activated, device cannot be deactivated.*

"Hell," Gabriel said. Looking up, he saw Millie looming over them, the pair of spears in hand once more. "Get her out of here. Take her to the plane and tell Rue to get the damn thing ready to fly."

"What are you going to do?"

"I don't know yet," Gabriel said. "But I've got to do something." He reached out for the nozzle, thinking maybe he could bend it backward or break it off, but the instant he touched it he discovered it was burning hot. He snatched his hand back, cursing.

"You can't stop it, Gabriel," Velda said in her suddenly affectless voice. "It's done. They'll pay for what they did to my father."

"I said get her out of here," Gabriel growled.

Millie reached for her. She shrank back, but he scooped her up in one big arm and dragged her to his chest. He looked her in the eye. "If you don't want what those two got, Velda, you'll come quietly. No biting, no hitting, no kneeing, no gouging. You try anything, you'll be out cold before you know it."

"Do you enjoy manhandling women," Velda said, struggling in his grip, "because your daddy gave you a sissy name?"

"No, ma'am," Millie said. "I like my name just fine. Now quiet down or I'll show you what real manhandling's like." He tightened his grip on her and headed off, ignoring her demands that he put her down and leaning on the spears in his other hand for support.

Gabriel turned back to the machine. If it couldn't be shut off, maybe it could at least be redirected? He took hold of the dial and turned it. The coordinates on the readout changed as he did so and he heard a grinding noise from the inside of the machine, as of some sort of internal mechanism laboriously being shifted to a new setting. So it wasn't too late for that: he could aim it at a different target.

But . . . what target? He'd turned the dial at random; he didn't recognize the new coordinates, didn't know what location he'd set it to. Somewhere in Eastern Europe, it looked like—maybe Russia. But he couldn't leave it there, obviously. The people there didn't deserve the destruction Velda had set in motion any more than the people of Berlin did. It was a Sophie's Choice he was facing, he realized, only on a monumental scale: to have to select not an individual but an entire city on earth to be destroyed.

Unless—

He was finding it hard to concentrate, hard to think at all, with the buzzing and the pain in his head, but he forced himself to focus.

Could he choose a location so remote, he thought, so unpopulated, that whatever effect this device had wouldn't hurt anyone—somewhere in the middle of a desert or the ocean, say?

It was an idea—but to make it work he'd need to know the coordinates of such a location, and he didn't. He knew the coordinates for plenty of places, but they were all places he'd been, and there wasn't one of them he'd be prepared to consign to destruction. There probably were some completely barren areas the Untergang device could target without harming anyone— the sort where governments conducted nuclear tests, for instance. But he was damned if he knew where they were, certainly not with the pinpoint accuracy that setting this machine required. He might be able to come close, to make a reasonable guess—but if he was off by a few degrees in specifying the coordinates, it could mean hundreds of thousands of lives. Or millions.

He looked over the notebook again. *Any deviation will reduce intensity in inverse proportion to the square of the distance . . .*

Maybe there *was* a way at least to choose a better rather than a worse target. Not by trying to decide what city deserved destruction, but by limiting the extent of the destruction itself. The Nazis had sent their mission here to the South Pole because this was apparently the perfect location from which to strike at Washington, D.C. A strike originating here that was directed at a different location would have "reduced intensity," Groener had written, with the reduction being greater as the target's distance from Washington increased. So the best possible place to strike if you wanted to do the least possible damage would be a location as far as possible from Washington, D.C. But where would that be?

He'd have been able to think more clearly if only his head hadn't been pounding and his vision hadn't been going blurry. It felt like his skull was being crushed in a wine press.

Where, damn it? Where could he direct the Untergang device to strike so it would do the least possible damage?

The answer came to him with sudden clarity.

He even had the coordinates.

He flipped back through the notebook, looking for a particular sentence he'd seen earlier.

Finding it, he turned the dial. His hand was shaking as he did so and his ears were ringing. The edges of his vision were not blurry any longer but blood red, and the borders of this red patch were encroaching on the center—it was as if he were looking at the world through a narrowing tunnel. But at the end of the tunnel he could still make out the panel showing the coordinates, and he kept working the dial until it reached the setting he wanted.

What was the farthest target from Washington, D.C.?

Right here.

To target Washington, device must be placed at precisely the following coordinates . . .

He got to his feet when the coordinates showing on the panel matched the ones shown in the notebook—the very spot where Gabriel was now standing. Let the

Untergang machine target itself. At minimum intensity, in the barren wastes of Antarctica—there weren't a lot of places less populated, certainly. That is, if you ignored this anomalous valley itself; even at minimum intensity, it might be irreparably damaged, maybe destroyed. But if he could get the people of the valley on the plane and make it out before the machine went off . . .

A new light flickered on above the coordinate panel, a bright yellow bulb that slowly blinked on and off. Then a man's voice, crackling with static, spoke, a recorded voice out of the distant past, perhaps Dr. Groener himself.

"Fünfzehn minuten zur aktivierung . . . Fünfzehn minuten zur aktivierung . . ."

Fifteen minutes to activation.

Not much time to load a half-century-old plane with two dozen hostile women, only one of whom spoke any English. Not to mention getting that plane in the air.

Which meant he had to leave *now*.

Gabriel turned to make his way out—and saw Velda storm through the doorway, Millie's two spears clutched in her hands.

Chapter 27

"Step away from that machine, Gabriel," Velda said, coming toward him. Her gown was in shreds, leaving her naked to the waist and barely covered below.

He didn't move. "What did you do to Millie?"

"Made him put me down," she replied flatly as she crossed the room, raising the spears to point at Gabriel's chest. "Remarkable what a kick to a broken ankle will do."

"You shouldn't have done it, Velda," Gabriel said. "He was taking you to safety. This place is going to be destroyed in minutes."

"*This* place? What are you talking about?" Her voice suddenly wasn't affectless anymore.

"I reset the device," Gabriel said. "To target itself."

"You did *what*?" Velda came to a stop.

"I can't let you kill millions of innocent people. No matter what the women here did to your father. Or what the Germans did to him sixty years ago."

"You had no right," she snarled. She jabbed one of the spears at him. He knocked its point aside with his forearm.

Velda lunged for him with the other spear, its sharpened stone blade whistling through the air directly toward his face. He ducked at the last second and it clanged against the metal sphere behind him. She pulled it back while stabbing out with the first spear again. It caught him high on one thigh, drawing blood.

He reached out, seized the shaft right behind the blade, and yanked it out of her grip. Spinning it in a circle like a staff, Gabriel brought the point around toward Velda. They faced off, weapons aimed at one another.

"Vierzehn minuten zur aktivierung . . ."

"If we don't get out of here, we're going to die," Gabriel said. "This thing's going off in fourteen minutes."

"So let me change the goddamn settings back, Hunt!" She swung her spear at his head. He tried to duck it, but the rapid motion of his head brought on a powerful wave of dizziness. He tried to stay upright, but couldn't. He put out one hand and caught himself as he tumbled to the floor. The spear fell from his grasp.

Velda was still standing. She was wincing, but she hadn't been in the room with the machine as long as he had, so she hadn't been affected as strongly yet. She strode forward, raising her spear high above her head with both hands, preparing to plunge it down into his neck.

"Don't, Velda," he said. He could barely hear his own voice over the thrumming of the machine and the rush of blood in his ears. "Please. Your father wouldn't want this sort of vengeance. His own daughter killing millions in his name? How could anyone who survived what he did want that?"

"Don't you dare presume to tell me what my father

would have wanted," Velda shouted, her eyes blazing with fury. "Don't you dare!" The silver pocket watch hung by its chain between her sweat-streaked breasts, its cover having snapped open as she ran. Inside, he saw the tiny photo, the older man and the loving daughter. She still saw herself as a loving daughter, he knew—but the savage hatred on her face now had nothing in common with the girl in the photo. Nothing in common with a sane human being.

If there had been more time, maybe he could have helped her, or someone could have; she could have recovered; this madness could have passed.

But there was no more time.

"Okay," Gabriel said, his voice soft. "Change it back. Do what you have to."

She lowered her spear and stepped forward. She was just a foot shy of the machine, and he was in the way. "Move," she said.

He tried to look her in the eye, but from where he lay she seemed miles away. "I'm sorry," Gabriel said. "I really am." And he rolled backward, hard, ramming with all his strength into the narrow metal legs of the frame that held the Untergang machine in place.

For an instant, the machine stayed where it was, just rotating as the structure beneath it tipped; the body of the sphere turned, the side with the heavy lens attached sliding down toward Gabriel and Velda, the side with the red-hot nozzle swinging up and out of reach. Then Gabriel rammed the frame again and the metal ball toppled from its perch.

Velda had time enough to raise one arm, as though to ward off a blow. The device plunged toward her. The thick, riveted metal skin narrowly missed her—and so did the heavy glass surface of the lens. They passed just inches away, the metal in front of her and the glass behind her. But any feeling of relief or triumph on her part must have been infinitely brief. Gabriel ducked his head and rolled out of the path of the sphere, so he didn't see what happened—but he heard the gruesome sizzle, saw the blinding flash of magnesium-white light, and smelled the strong, nauseating scent of ozone. When he looked back, she was gone.

The device itself rolled till it fetched up against the wall. The nozzle, miraculously, was still attached, still protruding from the sphere like a stem from an orange. The lens had snapped off and lay in pieces on the floor. Painted in soot across the surface of the largest piece he saw the silhouette of a woman, head thrown back, one arm raised above her head.

"Good-bye, Velda," he whispered as he staggered to his feet.

Was there any chance the thing was irreparably damaged, that it wouldn't go off . . . ? Any hope he might have harbored was dashed when he heard the crackly recorded voice, still counting down.

"Zwölf minuten zur aktivierung . . ."

Twelve minutes. He grabbed the spear he'd dropped and raced out of the room.

His head began clearing as soon as he got out into the open air. It was sticky, it was hot, it was humid—but it wasn't filled with deadly radiation or that intense, unnatural, unbearable pressure the machine had somehow created. He oriented himself quickly and headed off in the direction of the plane. He couldn't hear the voice any longer, but he knew what it would be saying: *zehn minuten . . . neun minuten . . . acht minuten . . .*

"Millie!" he called as he ran, pushing branches and enormous fronds out of the way. "Millie!"

"I'm here," came a pained reply a hundred yards later, and as Gabriel rounded a bend he saw the big man crawling toward him on his hands and knees, his face a mask of pure agony. The splint was still on his ankle, but the foot was bent crookedly inside it. Gabriel threw the spear to him and Millie reached up to snatch it out of the air. Gabriel rushed over to his side and helped him up. Millie leaned heavily on the spear and slung his other arm around Gabriel's shoulders. He stood on one leg, kept the other bent at the knee. He couldn't put any weight at all on it.

"Where's Velda?" Millie whispered through his grimace.

"She's dead," Gabriel said.

"Feel better already," Millie muttered.

"Bad news is, we'll be joining her if we don't get to that plane in ten minutes or less." He thought for a second. "Less."

"Seriously?" Millie said.

"Seriously," Gabriel said.

"Fuck." Millie took a deep breath. "All right. Let's do it."

They ran—or anyway Gabriel ran, as best he could with Millie's weight bearing down on his shoulders. The big man hopped along on one leg, planting the foot of the spear in the dirt each time and using it to pull himself forward with enormous heaves. The foliage grew thicker around them, slapping them in the face and chest as they lunged through it. But they kept pushing forward. Gabriel's heart was hammering and his breath was painful and ragged when they finally glimpsed the H-shaped tail fin between two trees up ahead.

"That's it," Gabriel said, "we're almost there—"

He heard a rustling in the undergrowth beside them. With a falling heart, he turned halfway around to face it. If it was another Tasmanian tiger, or god forbid one of those birds . . .

But when Millie, balancing on one leg, used the butt end of the spear to push aside a screen of leaves, Gabriel saw it hadn't been an animal making the noise. Crouched low to the ground, her half-strung beads clutched tightly between her hands, was the young girl from the village.

"Oh, god," Gabriel said. He looked back toward the village. The top of the tall central building was still in view, and as he watched, it crumpled inward.

He thought of the two unconscious guards he'd left behind on the floor. He thought of the old women by the well, who'd disappeared to who knew where. He thought of the pitiful sufferers in the men's tent. Even if Gabriel and Millie made it to the plane, even if Rue managed to get them off the ground, there'd be no shortage of death in this valley.

Not this one, too.

"Come on," he said to the girl, knowing she couldn't understand a word. She shrank away from him.

"Millie, you do it. Talk to her."

"I don't speak their—"

"Just *talk*, you goddamn horse whisperer," Gabriel said, and Millie steeled himself, forced the pain off his face and out of his voice, and began talking to the girl, low and soft, his words a trickle of sweet, slow molasses. "Come here, beautiful, it's okay, we're not gonna hurt you, you'll be okay—but you've got to come with us, that's it, come here . . ."

Gabriel looked back at the village again. The central building was completely gone, and a hot wind had started to blow in their direction, rattling the branches of the trees.

"Come on, Millie," Gabriel whispered. "Now or never."

The girl had crept forward. She was within reach. "I can't carry her and walk," Millie said.

"Put her on your back," Gabriel said.

"Honey, don't run, I'm gonna pick you up, you understand me?" He made a lifting gesture with his arm. "Up, okay? It'll be fine, just trust me." Gabriel looked in the girl's eyes. She seemed a bit less frightened, or at least he told himself she did.

"Now, Millie. Now."

With one sweep of his arm, Millie lifted the girl off her feet and tossed her onto his back. She squealed with momentary terror, but he kept talking to her, and when he let go of her skinny waist she didn't jump off. Instead, she wrapped her legs around his thick neck and took fistfuls of his hair in both little hands.

"That's great, honey," Millie said, "now we're going for a ride." And sweeping the spear out in front of him, he resumed his lurching forward march, Gabriel running alongside him, keeping him up.

The hot wind pursued them, gaining strength. It felt like it had reached gale force by the time they finally broke out into the clearing where the plane stood. A loud buzz of exclamations arose from the crowd of women when they saw Millie and Gabriel stagger into view with the wind at their back. Rue looked up. She was crouched on the plane's wing, twisting a wrench in the innards of the fuselage, but she leapt down and ran to them, pushing taller bodies out of the way till she was at Millie's other side and could grab him around the waist.

Looking down, Gabriel saw that one of Rue's small bare feet was wrapped with bloody barkcloth.

"Jesus," Gabriel said.

"Don't worry," Rue said. "It's not my clutch foot."

She steered them toward the open ramp at the rear of the plane.

"Have you got it working?" Gabriel asked.

"Like a charm," Rue said. "A cranky, leaky, rusty, sixty-five-year-old charm."

"Well, you've got five minutes to get us in the air," Gabriel said.

Rue's face couldn't properly be said ever to go pale, but she blanched all the same. "Five minutes . . . ?"

"*Fünf minuten*," Gabriel said. "Not a *minuten* more."

The women crowded all around them fell silent then, and stepped to either side. In the gap that opened up, Anika came forward. She had a vintage Luger in her hand, the German pistol aimed directly at Millie's gut. Apparently Groener's notebook hadn't been the only artifact of the Third Reich left around here.

"Lady, move," Millie said. To which Gabriel added, "If you don't let us up that ramp, Anika, we'll all die."

Her grip on the gun didn't waver.

"The Untergang machine," Gabriel said, then started over. "Unterg. Unterg has been activated. Turned on. Made angry. Look." He pointed back toward the trees, which were waving wildly in the wind. "Your main building—it's gone. Gone. Everything will be gone a few minutes from now. Everything—you, me, everything, if you don't let us get on this plane. If you don't let us take you away on the Father Bird."

"We cannot . . . ride the Father Bird," Anika said. "It is forbidden." But Gabriel saw her looking past him, over his shoulder, toward the village, and thought maybe he heard a bit of uncertainty in her voice.

"We have to go," he said. "Now, or everyone you care about will die. You and all your people. We can save you, but only if we go *right now*."

The girl, who was still sitting on Millie's shoulders, picked this moment to speak up.

Gabriel couldn't understand what she said in her piping little soprano voice; perhaps something about how they'd picked her up and brought her safely out of the forest. Perhaps something else entirely. But at the end of it, Anika's hand slowly descended.

"It *is* forbidden," she said, unhappily.

"First time for everything," Rue said and steered Millie up the ramp with her.

Gabriel stayed at its foot a moment longer. "Tell them to get on board as quickly as they can. Up there." He pointed at the plane's interior. "We're leaving in four minutes, with them or without them." Anika repeated the instructions to the throng of women and they began rushing up the ramp. Gabriel went ahead of them and pointed them to seats on padded benches against each wall. He opened a set of ancient supply lockers along the walls, one by one, disgorging parkas, blankets, and assorted other cold weather gear.

"Do we have enough fuel to make it to the nearest station?" Gabriel asked.

"Barely," Rue replied from the cockpit. "We'll be flying on fumes and Hail Marys."

"Is that a yes or a no?"

"It's an I'll do my best."

It would have to do.

Gabriel returned to his search of the cavernous hollow interior of the plane. He found stacks of tanned furs, skins of water, and baskets of desiccated fruit and dried meat—decades of offerings to the Father Bird, no doubt. He also found a complement of flight suits that had lain untouched for over sixty years.

"Anika, is everyone on board?" Gabriel said.

The older woman looked from face to face, tallying the confused and anxious women sitting half naked on the benches, and nodded. "All in."

"Tell them to bundle up in those furs," Gabriel told her, as he began pulling on one of the flight suits. "You too. You have no idea how cold it is where we're going."

Anika looked at Gabriel as if he'd lost his mind but did as he requested.

"Millie," Gabriel said, tossing him the largest of the suits. The big man was seated sprawled across the floor beside the cockpit. "Put some clothes on." Gabriel threw the smallest of the flight suits through the open door of the cockpit. "Rue, when are you going to start those engines?"

There was a growling sputter and cough before he finished getting the words out, and looking through the cockpit windows he saw the antique propellers struggling into motion like old men getting out of bed. The stench of thick smoky exhaust was overwhelming.

He returned to the center of the cabin, took one last look around the clearing through the still-open ramp at the back of the plane.

What he saw terrified him. The wind was strong enough now that the trees in its path were bent almost horizontal, the ones that hadn't already snapped off and been blown away. As he watched, the ground itself began to tremble, then to twist and hump like a living thing. *This was* minimum *intensity? Good lord—what would have happened to D.C. at the maximum level?*

He felt the plane grind into motion along the runway and saw the ramp slowly rise, laboriously drawing shut.

Then, suddenly there was an awful, unnatural sound, like a thick piece of metal being shredded. The surface of the runway seemed to shimmer with the same sort of distortion he'd seen beneath the giant lens of the Untergang machine. Gabriel felt the terrible pressure return, squeezing his skull painfully, and he saw the women around the cabin holding their heads in torment. As the plane's nose tipped up and its belly left the ground, a hot wave of fire struck them from behind, shoving them violently into the air. Gabriel was thrown against the side of one of the lockers and held on tight to prevent himself from being flung all the way into the cockpit.

"Rue, you okay?" he shouted.

"Don't talk to me," she shouted back.

The metal of the plane's body was screaming from the pressure, the velocity, the heat. Above them, the red dome of ice seemed to glow, the frozen fire coming to life as the furious heat from below began to melt the dome away, layer by layer. In the middle distance, he could see the narrow rift in the ice toward which they flew, and through it the slash of clean, white daylight beyond.

They were rushing toward it at ferocious speed—but they weren't there yet.

Gabriel pressed his face against the glass of a window and looked down. The ground continued to rapidly drop away beneath them, but that was the least of what he saw.

It was as if the entire valley below was being crumpled

like a used paper napkin in a giant's hand. The ground seemed to double up and fold in on itself, twisting and crushing everything in a rough spiral pattern radiating outward from the clearing where the machine had been. As Gabriel watched, appalled, the mesmerizing spiral suddenly collapsed inward, and a spout of churning, steaming lava gushed like blood from the torn earth.

"Lava at three o'clock," he shouted.

"I told you," Rue shouted back, "don't talk to me!" The plane suddenly lurched, as she turned the heavy-bodied craft nearly on end and steered it in a sharp turn away from the deadly flow.

Gabriel found himself flung from one side of the plane to the other, his fall softened only from landing on the bodies of half a dozen young women all wrapped up in furs and blankets. He made apologies uselessly—incomprehensibly, to them. At least there didn't seem to be any new broken bones, though he hated to think what Rue's maneuver might have done to Millie's ankle.

Out the nearest window, Gabriel saw the cliffs at the valley's edges begin to shudder and collapse. Cracks appeared and widened in the ice ceiling above. The ancient plane was vibrating all over as if about to shake itself to pieces.

"Hang on to something," Rue shouted from the cockpit. "It's gonna be a tight squeeze."

There was a deafening crunch as one of the wing tips smashed against the edge of the crack in the ice dome. For a terrible moment, Gabriel was afraid they were going down, but Rue fought with the controls and somehow held the plane steady.

The temperature inside the main cabin suddenly plummeted, dropping a hundred degrees in forty seconds. It left Gabriel gasping and shivering. The flight suit helped, but only so much; for one thing, his feet were still bare. And Rue couldn't be doing any better, especially with the wounds she'd endured. He grabbed an armful of skins and raced into the cockpit with them, dumping them on Rue's shoulders and lap. Freeing one hand at a time from the controls, she pulled them tightly around her.

"Thanks," she said, her teeth chattering.

"Can I talk to you now?" Gabriel said.

"No," Rue said. "But you can huddle with me for warmth."

Gabriel climbed into the seat beneath her and pulled the furs back over them both. She was freezing, but then so was he; together at least they stood a chance.

Glancing back, he saw that the faces of the women in the cabin were pale with shock, their eyes huge and unable to process what was happening, their bodies shivering pitifully with the brutal cold. The little girl was clinging tightly to Millie, her arms too short to protrude from the sleeves of the parka in which he'd zipped her up.

"Anika," Gabriel said, shouting to be heard over the roar of the engines. "Tell them to huddle together, to hold tight to each other. It's the only way they'll survive this flight." He heard Anika saying something and saw Millie gesturing.

They'd figure it out. They'd have to.

"How much longer till we land?" Gabriel asked Rue. "How far to Pole Station?"

"Which do you want to know?" she said, concentrating on correcting for chop. The turbulence was exceptional.

"What do you mean?" Gabriel asked.

"Pole Station is quite a ways off," she said. "But with that engine gone, we won't be in the air for long enough to reach it." She nodded toward the right side of the cockpit, where Gabriel saw that one of the giant propellers was not turning. As he stared, the second one on that side sputtered to a stop.

Rue flipped an old toggle switch on the control panel. Her voice boomed out of a loudspeaker behind them. "Attention passengers, this is your captain speaking. We are beginning our descent into beautiful downtown nowhere."

She flipped the switch again, tried to look through the iced-over cockpit windows, then gave up and peered at the instruments. "This isn't the way I wanted to go," she said. "Frozen solid at the South Pole."

"Oh?" Gabriel said, forcing a grin onto his trembling lips. "How did you want to go?"

"Heart attack," she said, "brought on by the biggest orgasm of my life."

"Well, don't give up on your dream just yet," Gabriel said. "If you put this bird down safely, we might still make it."

"That's what I love about you, Gabriel," Rue said. "You're such a goddamn optimist."

The plane was wracked with a huge blow, as if they'd been swatted by a tremendous club.

"Hang on, optimist," Rue muttered, "we're going down."

Gabriel had been through some hairy landings in the past, but none of them could compare to the vicious turbulence of this one or the blast of freezing wind that enveloped them as the plane began to come apart at the seams. They plowed into the snow, wings snapping and propellers flying off in every direction. The passengers in the cabin were thrown and scattered. And Gabriel himself was flung through the air. He saw a heavy metal panel loom before him, jutting from the snow. Then he hit it face-first, and blackness swallowed everything.

Chapter 28

When he regained consciousness, he was in a cramped chamber along with Rue, Millie, the two dozen women, and two bearded scientists who kept looking around them with incredulous expressions.

"You mind telling us who the hell you-all are?" the older of the two scientists asked, his voice laced with a tawny Tarheel accent.

Gabriel tried to sit up on the army cot on which he'd been laid out. He gave up after a few attempts.

"That a *Nazi* plane you were flying?" the younger one said.

"Yes," Gabriel said, his voice hoarse. "It's a long story."

"Well, that's fine with us," the older scientist said. "We've got all the time in the world, don't we?" And the younger one chuckled and nodded, as though at an inside joke.

"What are you talking about? Where are we?" Gabriel turned his head painfully to look out the frost-coated window on his left and saw just a razor sliver of orange sun hovering above the distant horizon.

"You're at the South Pole, son," the older scientist said. "Pole Station. We saw the fire from your engines and went out to haul you in. You know, we don't normally get a lot of visitors dropping in out here. Specially not lovely young women dressed in scraps of fur and nothing else."

"In a Nazi plane," the younger one muttered. It seemed to be the point he was fixated on.

"Although if we did," the older one went on, "we might not have such a problem getting staff to sign up for winter-over."

"Winter-over?" Rue said, suddenly alert. "When's the last flight out?"

"About two and a half hours ago," the older scientist said. "There won't be another flight in or out of here for six months."

Everyone fell silent.

"So, you see," the older one said, "we have plenty of time to listen to a long story."

"What the hell are we supposed to do up here for six months?" Millie said, then checked himself. Gabriel saw him looking at the crowd of women around him. "You think they'll still expect me to . . . ?"

"To do your duty by them," Gabriel said. "I don't see why not."

Rue caught Gabriel's gaze and shook her head slowly. "Just so long as you remember where *your* duty lies," she said. "You and me, we've got a little matter of a death wish to explore."

"Excuse me?" the younger scientist said.

Gabriel closed his eyes.

It was going to be an interesting six months.

And now—a sneak preview of the next
Gabriel Hunt adventure:

Hunt Among the
Killers of Men

Prologue

The sign was in eleven languages including Arabic, German, Dutch, English, Russian, and both Mandarin and Cantonese variants for the locals. The English interpretation read:

The Chinese Cooperative Confederation
Welcomes Its Honored Guests
(private reception)

In any language the message was clear: *Keep Out*.

If this polite suggestion was vague, the men keeping watch over all ingress and egress were heavy with implied threat. They were all uniformed members of the People's Armed Police Force, carrying the authority of the Central Military Committee. Dressed in tightly belted army greens, they bore both sidearms and automatic weapons; in comportment they looked the same as the officer directing the hectic traffic mere blocks away, not far from the world-famous bronze statue of Mao Tse-Tung pointing boldly toward the future. The statue still stood outside the Peace Hotel on the Bund, though Mao's historical significance had lately been overshadowed by the political and economic reforms of his successors.

At night the Bund is brilliant with golden light, presently competing with an ever-increasing array of garish neon advertisements in all languages. The most unusual building found on the Bund sits in Pudong Park in Lujiazui. It is called "the Pearl"—short for the Oriental Pearl TV Tower. It looks like a recently landed spaceship from another planet. A massive tripod base supports three nine-meter-wide columns of stainless steel that encase a variety of metallic spheres and globes. The topmost globe, at an elevation of nearly 1,500 feet, is called the "space module." From the large lower sphere, one can see all the way to the Yangtze River. The design aesthetic was to create "twin dragons playing with pearls," derived from the presence of the Yangpu Bridge to the northeast and the Nanpu Bridge to the southwest.

The Pearl is home to commerce, recreation, and history. The Shanghai Municipal History Museum is housed in its pedestal. The topmost sphere features a revolving restaurant. In between are shops, more restaurants, hotel facilities and the transmission headquarters for nearly two dozen television channels and FM radio stations. The Pearl is so dominant on the Bund that it can be seen from twenty miles inland; lit up at nighttime, it is a truly eerie, otherworldly sight.

Zhongshan Road was seething with traffic—everything from skate-sized diesel automobiles to pedicabs and bicycles (thousands of bicycles)—binding and blending with pedestrians (thousands more). Every twenty minutes the Sin Shan Ferry brought more people, more vehicles. A roiling, complex sea of humanity.

At night the abundance of artificial light from the

Bund, and from the Pearl, makes the Huangpu River appear almost black.

Qingzhao Wai Chiu, whose given name meant "clear illumination and understanding," understood appearances and how to manipulate them. Klaxons sounded for the docking ferry, and she debarked, pulling her little wheeled suitcase behind her.

There was a beggar trying to negotiate the upward slope of the ferry ramp. It was a legless old woman, hauling herself along on a wheeled platform by means of wooden blocks, totally alone on the concrete ramp until the steel mesh gates withdrew and the complement of ferry passengers surged toward her in an unbroken wave. She kept her eyes down, as is common for beggars. Inevitably her cup was jostled and a few meager coins pinwheeled down the ramp or disappeared beneath the shoes of the incoming.

The disparity between the old wretch and Qingzhao could not have been more striking. Qingzhao was tall for a Chinese woman—five foot nine, rendered even taller by expensive spike heels so new the soles were barely scuffed. Unlike many women, she knew how to walk in those heels. Her stride itself could be a weapon, a statement. Her full, lush fall of ebony-black hair concealed many scars. Her gaze could be as steely dark as espresso but it was shielded now behind tinted glasses. She walked with a purpose.

She tucked a one hundred-yuan note into the beggar's cup, noticing the depth of the ragged woman's platform. It was designed to conceal her lower legs. She was a fake. She looked skyward and off-center at the sound of paper rustling in the cup and Qingzhao saw her milky, cataracted eyes. She probably was not really blind, either. No matter. Qingzhao was faking, too.

The beggar was swallowed by the crowd as Qingzhao made her way toward the rocketship, the TV tower—the Pearl.

The policemen flanking the sign ate her up head-to-toe with expressions just shy of leering. She knew what they were thinking: *An entertainer, probably a prostitute.* That was what she needed them to think.

First hurdle cleared.

In the Tower lobby there was more security on behalf of the reception for the CCC—double guards and a walk-through booth twice the size of an airport scanner. Qingzhao knew this was a recently emplaced piece of Japanese technology that could present a body scan in X-ray schematic.

The scan of her trolley case revealed that it contained, among other things, a flamboyant, metallic wig—the sort of thing a dancer might wear. Or a stripper.

The guards made her open the case anyway, mostly so they could sneak peeks down her cleavage. Her silk blouse and leather jacket had been strategically chosen and just as strategically deployed. These baboons would never see the big X of scar tissue beneath her left breast, or care.

Qingzhao was waved toward a lift with brushed aluminum doors. The car shot up nearly a thousand feet in fifteen seconds; she felt her ears pop.

Second hurdle cleared.

The Chinese Cooperative Confederation was the brainchild of a financier who had changed his name to Kuan-Ku Tak Cheung, although Qingzhao knew the man was Russian by birth. It represented a new sociopolitical horizon for twenty-first-century China, which irritated all the traditionalists and old Party members but represented an enticing commercial future for China's so-called new generation. As far as the old school was concerned, giving Cheung a political foothold would be akin to the Mafia fielding a presidential candidate in the United States. But it did not really matter as long as the correct palms were silvered. And Cheung, ever the tactician, was perpetually developing inroads to curry the favor of his harshest opponents.

Of course, politics had nothing to do with the reasons Qingzhao had come to kill Cheung, whose real name was Anatoly Dragunov.

The noise level was painfully high in the middle of the Moire Club, overlooking the Huangpu from the mid-section of the Pearl.

On a revolving chromium stage, expressionless dancers in white bodystockings and face-paint moved like robots, tracking the gyrations of naked men and women being projected onto them from hidden lenses.

At least five hundred guests and noteworthies were portioned into pie-wedge areas sectioned by hanging panes of soundproof karaoke glass. In the midst of chaos, silence could be had. The glass was also bullet-proof, grade six, arranged to accommodate any sized group and isolate them in plain sight. Each alcove of glass was a different projected color. The support wires could also transmit billing information from any of the glass-topped scanner tables.

The servers were all *Takarazuka*—female Japanese exotics dressed as tuxedoed men, supervised by a matron dolled up in an elaborate fringed gown and a mile-high pile of spangled hair, himself a transplant from a Dallas, Texas, drag show where he had specialized in Liza Minnelli.

At the maître d' station there was another body

scanner. Even an amateur could have picked out guest from bodyguard. The watchdogs were too confident, too arrogant, too chest-puffy. They had seen too much Western television and been inspired by too many Western films.

Ivory was disappointed by this crew, but it was not his place to say so. His job was not only to watch the crowd, but to watch the watchers. He was a dark-haired, sharp-eyed son of Heilongjiang Province—although those records had been erased long ago. His current name was Longwei Sze Xie—nickname, "Ivory," source unknown—and he looked like he was in charge of everything.

An immaculate, six-foot blonde Caucasian woman had just raised the hackles of the mâitre d' at the scanner. She was packing a sleek .380 in a spine retention holster just below the elaborate calligraphy of the tattoo on the small of her back. Vistas of exposed flesh, yards of leg, a good weight of ample bosom, and yet she could still artfully hide a firearm inside the slippery, veiled thing she was almost wearing.

Ivory quickly interceded: "She's one of Cheung's." Meaning: *Her gun is permitted.* Just like the similar gun concealed amidst the charms of her opposite number, an equally statuesque African goddess named Shukuma—Cheung's other arm doily for the evening.

Kuan-Ku Tak Cheung, a.k.a. Anatoly Dragunov, was holding forth from a VIP area near the center of the swirling carnival. Ivory put the man to be in his mid-fifties; barrel chest, huge hands, a face like unfinished sculpture. From his vantage Ivory could see that Shukuma had Cheung's back at all times. Good. Either she or the blonde, Vulcheva, would signal if Ivory needed to be called into play.

Down in the VIP pit, Cheung placed a denominational bill on the glass table before each of his honored guests, four in focus: Japanese yen for Mr. Igarishi, a new Euro for Mr. Beschorner, modern rubles for Mr. Oktyabrina, and good old U.S. of A. dollars for Mr. Reynaldo.

Mr. Igarishi said, "We are equally honored." He spoke with a Kyoto inflection.

Cheung said, "I respect the charm of a gesture." Turning to Beschorner, he added, "True wealth is invisible, ja?" in Frankfurt German. To Mr. Oktyabrina he added, "Ones and zeros are what we are really after," and completed the sentence in English for the benefit of Mr. Reynaldo: ". . . so we cannot deny the purity." He had just delivered an unbroken speech in four languages. He was showing off. They were all multilingual. But it helped to choose a negotiative tongue that could not be readily comprehended by, say, the average waiter.

"Paper currency is almost extinct," he told his familiars. "What you see is the last gasp of that outmoded idiom, and I guarantee it will pass muster anywhere in the world. Paper currency will erect our economical siege machine. In the aftermath of what we do, digital currency will make us all wealthy beyond the belief of ordinary human beings."

"*If* you can deliver China as promised," said Beschorner.

"I anticipate all phases complete within the next two years," said Cheung.

Ivory monitored all this via earbud. New dancers, tricked out in painfully complex PVC fetishwear, had taken the circular chrome stage.

Then somebody opened fire on Cheung, Ivory's

boss, and people started diving for cover. Except for Ivory, still standing, eyes unfazed, gun already drawn.

Qingzhao quickly approached the backstage corral as the white-bodystockinged dancers hustled off. She smiled as her "fellow performers" passed. Half of them returned her expression, no doubt thinking: *What was her name again? I'm sure I've met her.* The men got deferential avoidance of eye contact, otherwise they might spend too much time later trying to place her face.

The hosed and goggled PVC outfits had been wheeled to the prep floor on a giant mobile rack whose casters creaked with the weight of the gear. All the evening's entertainments had been either calculatedly androgynous or garishly sexual, and Qingzhao could advantage either opportunity as it arose. The next troupe went on in another ten minutes.

The only privacy backstage was found in the staff toilets. Performers had a splendid nonchalance about nudity, which meant that Qingzhao could use her breasts, ass and million-watt smile as further distractions from the fact that she was not supposed to be there at all. She stripped off her wrap skirt, her jacket, her blouse, while striding purposefully toward her destination. On the way, she lifted one of the PVC costumes from the rack.

In the loo she cracked open her little wheeled suitcase. The wig inside matched the gear for the PVC dancers.

After opening the case handle, popping the hidden seam on the heavy-duty hinges, and unclicking a concealed hatch on the wig mount, Qingzhao assembled the components for her pistol—a big AutoMag IV frame jazzed up to resemble the prop space guns that were also part of the forthcoming presentation. A steel tube disgorged a full magazine's worth of specialty ammunition. They were heavy-caliber loads with black and yellow hazard striping on the cartridge casings.

Miraculously, the assembled gun actually fit the holster that was part of the stage costume—an unanticipated plus, there.

The white facial pancake and black lipstick and liner she rapidly applied made her indistinguishable from the others, male or female. This, she had counted on.

Feeling like an ingénue in a chorus line, she filed onstage with the rest, having no idea whatsoever about marks, timing, position, or the number to which they were supposedly herky-jerking around. It did not matter. She needed five seconds, tops, before she was blown.

Outside the Pearl, a dirigible bloated with neon circled the convex windows.

In a single liquid move, Qingzhao pivoted, crouched, sighted and fired.

The bullet rocketed across the room and hit the plexi about a foot away from Kuan-Ku Tak Cheung's head. The tempered material spiderwebbed but did not shatter. The round left a broad, opaque splatter like a paintball round.

Which began to effervesce. Acid.

Immediately, Ivory, Shukuma and Vulcheva triangulated to shield Cheung, guns out.

The highly paid bodyguards of Cheung's international guests lacked such reaction time. They were still unholstering their weaponry and trying to acquire a target. By the time they found their senses, Qingzhao had fired twice more.

The compromised plexi disintegrated and the unfortunate Mr. Igarishi took a round in the head that nearly vaporized his skull.

Ivory brought up his pistol in a leading arc and returned auto-rapidfire through the breached glass singlehandedly—something not many men could do with a sense of control. The OTs-33 "Pernach" in his grasp stuttered, instantly reducing its double-stack 27-round mag by half in the first burst. "Pernach" meant "multivaned mace" in Russian, and a jagged line of Parabellum rounds chased Qingzhao's wake as she dived off the stage.

Ivory did not pause in astonishment as Qingzhao hit the circular lip of the stage, shooting back while in midfall. He already knew how capable she was.

Vulcheva's shooting arm violently parted company with her body, the spray causing everyone to duck. The hanging plexi all around the club was jigging now with bullet hits as other enforcers tried to determine what threat, from where, and filled the night with panic fire.

Ivory broadsided Cheung and caught two hits in the chest. He did not go down. It took him less than a tenth of a second to register the acid and he quickly stripped his jacket, which was lined with whisper-thin body armor of Japanese manufacture. Spotlights exploded above him.

Ivory and Shukuma bulldogged Cheung into the body scanner at the mâitre d' station. Ivory hit the device's panic button, which dropped chainmail-style rollups to enclose his boss. Cheung's skeleton showed on the screen in blue, but no bullet could harm him there. The less-lucky mâitre d' was slumped across the dais, having interrupted the travel of several conventional rounds fired by other bodyguards.

Ivory only had eyes for Qingzhao, who was now boxed in near the panoramic windows with no place to run. The blimp cruised past behind her, flashing advertising in polyglot: *CortCom. Vivitrac. Eat Nirasawa-Mega-Output Beverage!*

Qingzhao brought an entire framework of glass panels down on Ivory's head. Then she put the rest of her clip into the big curved window, which disassembled itself and succumbed to gravity.

Ivory had her dead in his sights as she jumped. He spent the rest of his clip trying to wing her on the way out.

He ran to the window, icy night air scything inward. From this high up, the light of the Bund made it impossible to see the river. No parachute, no falling body, just blackness.

Qingzhao, Ivory knew, would have counted on that.

Chapter 1

"I give up."

Gabriel Hunt was widely known for solving mysteries and rising to challenges. This time, however, frustration had bested him.

"I give up. You do it."

He relinquished the Rubik's Cube, placing it onto the table (itself a Chinese antique gifted by a beneficiary of a Hunt Foundation grant) next to a more obscure and even more difficult puzzle called the Alexander Star.

"It's a toy, Gabriel. Children do it."

"So give it to a child then," Gabriel said.

Michael picked the cube up, began idly turning its sides. Instead of colors, each square was labeled with a piece of the Hunt Foundation logo against a different metallic background—silver, copper, bronze, gold—and the toy itself was made of stainless steel rather than plastic. "You give up on things too quickly," he said. In his hands, the facets slowly assembled themselves.

"Name one thing I've given up on," Gabriel said. "Just one. Other than this toy."

"The Dufresne report."

"I brought back the mask. Dufresne should be happy."

"He wants a report."

"Here's your report: I brought back the mask, close quotes, signed, Gabriel Hunt. What else does he want to know?"

Michael shook his head. "He has a board of trustees he has to answer to. It's not enough to hand him a carton and say, here, here's your mask. That's not the way things are done in the foundation world. You should know that."

Why was it that every time Michael opened his mouth, he sounded like he was the older brother rather than the younger? Gabriel was his senior by six years and change.

Michael set down the Rubik's Cube, its sides neatly arranged, entropy defeated once again.

"Never mind," he said, heaving a familiar sigh. "I'll write it."

"Make it good," Gabriel said. "Tell them I had to sneak past a tribe of cannibals to get it."

"In the south of France?"

"Gourmet cannibals."

"I'd appreciate it, Gabriel, if you could show a modicum of seriousness about these things."

"I know you would, Michael. It's what I love about you. You use words like 'modicum' with a straight face."

They were a study in contrast, Gabriel and his brother.

Both were still in tuxedos—how often had *that* fate befallen them?—the evening's entertainment having consisted of the Hunt Foundation's annual Martin J.

Beresford Memorial Awards dinner two floors below. But where Michael wore his bespoke tailored suit with quiet dignity, Gabriel had untied the bowtie and cummerbund of his rented number and undone the shirt studs halfway down his chest. Michael was scholarly, almost tweedy, bespectacled; the pallor of his skin reflected a life spent largely indoors, these days behind a computer screen much of the time, or else talking on the telephone to similarly pale men halfway around the globe. Gabriel was darker—hair as black as shoe crème, skin browned by the sun of many lands. He was chiseled, the muscles of his long arms ropy. The last time he'd found himself behind a computer he'd been using the thing as a shield. You can't beat a nice solid IBM laptop for stopping a bullet.

The aegis of the Hunt Foundation had made both brothers moderately famous in their respective ways, and to an extent they depended on one another for their success. Gabriel's discoveries in the field and unearthments of historical significance would not have been possible without the Foundation's financial support. Michael, in turn, acknowledged grudgingly that much of the Foundation's prestige derived from the attention Gabriel's higher-profile successes had brought in—the kind of risk-taking that is indefensibly reckless until it yields something suitable for publication.

"Your presentation went over well," Michael said in a conciliatory tone.

"It had pictures. Everyone likes pictures."

"Oh, you're in one of your *moods*," Michael said.

"Four hours of speeches from guys in penguin suits will put anyone in a mood. Anyone but you."

"Maybe so." Michael sorted through some of the neatly arranged papers on the table, pulled a sheet and turned it to face Gabriel. "Before you go." He uncapped a fountain pen and held it out. "You still have to cosign the endowment for the Indonesian group." All significant expenditures of the Hunt Foundation needed to bear the signatures of both brothers, though Michael handled all other aspects of the organization's administration on his own.

"The Molucca figures," said Gabriel. "Right." He reached out for the pen, and at that moment both brothers heard the sound of footsteps outside the office door. The knob turned, the door swung toward them, and a member of the Foundation staff stuck his head inside. "Mr. Hunt?"

"Yes?" Michael said. "What is it, Roger?"

But Roger said, "Not you, sir," and turned to Gabriel.

"Me?"

"There's a woman, sir, asking for you. Quite . . . informally dressed. She insists on speaking with you. I let her know you were occupied with Foundation business, but she insisted she has something of utmost importance to discuss with you . . . in private, sir."

"Do you know who this is, Gabriel?" Michael asked. "Some old paramour of yours?"

"Probably," Gabriel said. "Though how any of them would know to look for me here I don't know."

"Possibly your last name on the plaque by the door," Michael said, "next to the word 'Foundation,' had something to do with it."

"Where is she?" Gabriel asked Roger.

"In the club room, sir." Roger's expression was unreadably neutral. He was very good at his job.

Gabriel bent over the Indonesian papers, signed them swiftly in triplicate, re-capped the pen and followed

Roger to the door. "Don't wait up for me," he told Michael.

"Oh, I know better than that," Michael said.

As Roger led him down a gently curving and lushly carpeted flight of stairs, Gabriel ran through in his head the women who could possibly have tracked him down here. Annabelle? Rebecca? No; they were both still in Europe and lacked visas to travel to the U.S. Joyce Wingard? Fiona Rush? Unlikely in the former case, strictly impossible in the latter. Then who? He could have continued guessing indefinitely without ever thinking of the woman who turned from the window at the far end of the room to face him after he entered the club room and shut the door behind him.

"Hello, Gabriel."

"Lucy?"

He saw her bristle at the name.

Lucy Hunt had been born Lucifer Artemis Hunt, thanks to parents whose knowledge of classical antiquity and Biblical scholarship exceeded their ability to anticipate the taunting a girl might be forced to endure from her peers if they named her Lucifer. They'd meant well, naming all three of their children after archangels from the Bible, but Gabriel and Michael had gotten the long end of that particular stick and Lucy the short. When she'd run away from home at age seventeen, her name hadn't been the cause, or at least not the sole cause—but all the same, she'd taken to calling herself Cifer. She'd also severed all ties to the family, the Foundation, and her prior life. Gabriel had seen her a grand total of two times in the past nine years, neither of them here in the building where they'd grown up; and he knew Michael hadn't seen her even once. He'd exchanged e-mail with the mysterious "Cifer" from time to time, but had no idea who it really was, because at Lucy's request Gabriel had never told him.

"What are you doing here?" Gabriel asked.

She came forward. She was wearing scuffed, mud-spattered sneakers and well-worn leather pants; a battered denim jacket with a black T-shirt underneath; and a canvas rucksack over one shoulder. She had obviously just thundered in out of the rain. Her wet hair was dyed brick red and chopped short, and she had a large Celtic tattoo Gabriel didn't remember decorating one side of her neck. She'd filled out a bit since Gabriel had seen her last, put on some weight that she'd badly needed; she was in her midtwenties now and quite pretty, and cleaned up she'd be a killer. But that was about as likely to happen, Gabriel knew, as a televangelist refusing a tithe.

She stopped beside him. "I can only stay a short time, Gabriel. I'm not even supposed to be in the country. I'm supposed to be under house arrest in Arezzo." She lifted one leg of her pants to reveal a bit of high-tech apparatus clamped around her ankle; a red LED on it flashed silently every few seconds. "I hacked it so it says I'm still there. But they do visual sweeps every three days, which only gives me till tomorrow night to get back."

"Jewelry-wise, you might want to go with something a bit more spidery," Gabriel said. "So I repeat, what are you doing here?"

"When I heard about Mitch, I had to come. She needs help. Which means I need *your* help." She took note of Gabriel's monkey suit, nodded toward it. "Hey. Business or funeral?" she said.

"Funeral would have been more fun," said Gabriel.

"Why I got the hell out," she muttered. "So, what about it? Talk?"

"Sure, what the heck? We can get Michael down here, make it a real family reunion. There's got to be some ice cream in a freezer around here someplace. Marshmallows. We can put on our pjs and talk all night."

"Serious," she said, shucking water like a cat. She took him by the wrist, tugged him toward the door.

"What's wrong with talking here? It's wet out there." But she kept tugging. "Fine." Gabriel grabbed an umbrella from an elephant-foot stand, buttoned up his shirt with his other hand. "After you," he said.

"I've got this friend, Mitch," Lucy began. "Short for Michelle."

She had steered Gabriel to a caffeine dive in the Village where the espresso ran extra-strong and the lights were kept mercifully low. On the way out of the townhouse, Gabriel had abandoned his suit jacket for a nicely broken-in A2, US Army Air Corps vintage circa 1942, with the emblem of the Eighth Air Force and the Flying Eight-Balls on one shoulder. He was still wearing the white piquet tuxedo shirt under it, though.

"Mitch is air force—or she was, before they threw her to the wolves for a helicopter crash, a training flight accident. They needed a scapegoat and wouldn't nail the pilot because of rank. Plus they hate the idea of a woman in the program, needless to say."

"Is this going to be another feminist soapbox thing?" said Gabriel. "Or does it get interesting?"

"Just shut up and listen and I'll get to it."

"Okay." Gabriel took another sip. The coffee here really was very good; the kind of drink that made you want to sit and contemplate deeper mysteries.

"So: Mitch gets defrocked. She comes back to New York to stay with her sister, Valerie, who works in the records department of a company called Zongchang Limited. But the day Mitch arrives, Valerie goes to a meeting with Zongchang's foreign corporate heads at a hotel. The police find her heels-up in a Dumpster at 1 A.M. the next day with the stale Caesar salad. Her throat's been cut, and she's been shot through the heart."

"Both?"

"Yeah—and that's not even the interesting part. Do the cops go hunting for someone who might have done it? No—they nail Mitch for it. For the murder of her own sister. No way in hell, but that's what they've decided. She Twittered it on the way to jail. I snuck myself onto the next flight over."

"Twittered?"

"It's a microblogging tool—think of it as a way you can update a blog from your cell phone—" She saw Gabriel's blank stare. "Never mind. Point is, she told me what was happening. They're only calling her a 'material witness' for now, but it's obvious they think she did it. The only good part of the whole thing is that, over the prosecutor's objections, the judge has set bail. Which by the way means I need some bail money."

"If what you want's money," Gabriel said, "Michael's got the checkbook."

"I can't ask him. Can you picture that, first time I see him in a decade, it's *Hey, Michael, can you get my friend out of jail? And by the by, I'm sort of under arrest myself . . .*" Lucy shook her head. "Anyway the money's not all I want. Listen. The high muckety-mucks in this company have something to do with 'ethnographic Chinese antiquities.'"

"I think I remember reading something about that,"

Gabriel said, "the head of Zongchang being a collector. Ching, or Chung, something like that."

"Yeah, well, Mitch is pretty sure Ching-or-Chung whacked her sister because she found out something she wasn't supposed to. But now the men who did it have hightailed it back to China—to the CCC. You know what that is?"

Gabriel pinched the bridge of his nose. The CCC. He knew this political movement-cum-Mafia only by ruthless reputation, since he had somehow managed to avoid a hands-on run-in with them. "The Chinese Co-operative Confederation. It's a lot like Russia after the Soviet Union fell apart. Like Morocco during World War Two."

"Bastards who play for keeps, was how Mitch put it," said Lucy. "They're outside international law. No extradition—"

"No diplomatic inquiry," said Gabriel, nodding.

"Once someone's tucked away in there, there's no getting them out."

"And you want to get someone out?"

"Mitch does. And unless they keep her locked up for the rest of her life, she's going to go after him herself. Neither of which is a great alternative. I mean, Mitch can take care of herself, but I wouldn't want to see her go up against an organization like this."

"Unlike me, for instance," Gabriel said.

Lucy nodded, and the look of utter confidence in her eyes shot right through Gabriel's defenses. It was like when she was eight years old and he was twenty, freshly back from a year in North Africa, and she'd listened to his exaggerated tales of his exploits with rapt attention each night after Michael had headed off to bed. She'd believed he could do anything. He'd believed it for a while himself.

"And who is this woman?" asked Gabriel. "Why is it so important to you to help her?"

Lucy paused before answering. "She's a friend," Lucy said. "I've known her a long time. She got me through some very bad stuff. I owe her a lot."

"All right," Gabriel said. He mulled over the possibilities. "The CCC," he said. "Well, moving around inside China's easier than it used to be, though you'd still want cover for something like this. One possibility, Michael was telling me about a lecture series he's setting up at a bunch of Chinese universities. He's supposed to give the lectures himself—but who'd really complain if I showed up with him?"

Lucy allowed herself the ghost of a smile. "Or instead of him. You'd really wake up some of those rooms."

"No doubt," Gabriel said. "So, tell me straight: what exactly is it you want me to do?"

"First thing is help me get Mitch out of jail," said Lucy. "And then convince her that she doesn't need to fly to China to kill this guy."

"Because I'll do it for her? I'm not some sort of assassin, Lucy."

"You'll think of something," Lucy said. "You always do."

DON'T MISS THE NEXT EXCITING ADVENTURE OF GABRIEL HUNT!